THE SEVEN DEADLY FEARS

by

Edward   Bear

M&J Publishing
P.O. Box 460516
Denver, CO 80246-0516

Other Books by Edward Bear:

The Dark Night of Recovery
The Seven Deadly Needs
The Cocktail Cart

Acknowledgements.
For permission to use the following selections,
grateful thanks are extended:
Harcourt, Brace & World: The Diary of Anais Nin,
Anais Nin, Vol.#3, 1966. J.P. Tarcher: The
Aquarian Conspiracy, Marilyn Ferguson, 1980.
Three Rivers Press: Satch Sez, Satchel Paige, 2000.
Modern Library: Basic Writings, C.G. Jung, 1993.
Harper Collins: The Sacrament of the Present
Moment, Jean Pierre de Caussade, 1989. Harper
Collins: A Return to Love, Marianne Williamson

Cover design by Sarah Edgell.
  sarah@edgellworks.com

Printed in the United States of America
First trade printing: May, 2002
Library of Congress Card Number: 2002103027

PUBLISHER'S NOTE
This is a work of fiction. Any resemblance to
persons, living or dead, events, or locales is
entirely coincidental.

Life shrinks and expands according to one's courage.
Anais Nin

Fear...was an evil and corroding thread; the fabric of our existence was shot through with it.
Bill W.

I've developed a new philosophy...I only dread one day at a time.
Charlie Brown

I'm devilishly afraid...but I'll sing that I may seem valiant.
John Dryden

Fear is sand in the machinery of life.
Miguel de Unamuno

Sometimes you win, sometimes you lose, sometimes you get rained out.
Satchel Paige

God instructs the heart not by ideas, but by pains and contradictions.
Jean Pierre de Caussade

We meet ourselves time and again in a thousand disguises on the path of life.
Carl Jung

Feed your faith and your fears will starve to death.
Anonymous

To:

*Jo, who hangs the moon and the stars
every night.*

*The Children, Tommy, Tree, Cat, Monica,
Laura & Steve.*

*The 7 A.M. York Street, Attitude Adjustment
Meeting.*

PROLOGUE

"Only the self-deceived will claim perfect freedom from fear."

Bill W.

"Fear causes so much trouble, it ought to be ranked with stealing."

Bill. W.

"Hey, it's me—Lamont Cranston, The Shadow."

That's the way he starts every conversation when he calls. "Hey, it's me—Lamont Cranston." Like there's only one "me" and I should certainly know who it is. Or who Lamont Cranston is. But by this time, of course, I do know; only it's not really Lamont Cranston, the mysterious Shadow of radio fame, but our very own, nearly senile, Tyler. At first he had to explain who Lamont Cranston was (commenting, as he always does, about my lack of education), who The Shadow was, then went on about the Green Hornet, Jack Armstrong, Fred Allen and the whole cast of radio characters he grew up listening to. Way more than I wanted to know. As you may have guessed, Tyler is an old person. A very old

1

person. Anyone who grew up listening to radio is, by definition, a very old person.

He is settling into what he calls the Last Few Innings (always the baseball guy) with all the grace of an elephant trying to get into a telephone booth. He's making a big production out of it, though he's trying very hard to make it appear effortless. He sees the Grim Reaper lurking behind every ache and pain. Death, he seems to be saying without actually saying it, is imminent. Approaching at the speed of light. He's the bravest of knights, he would have us believe—stoic and heroic. But then he's been saying that for a long time. About dying. Possibly since he was young, though I didn't know him then. He is at least twenty years older than I am (I'm forty-five), and I honestly believe he will outlive me. We'll probably have to drive a stake through his heart when the time comes.

"So how long has it been since we taped all that stuff about *The Seven Deadly Needs*?" he wants to know.

"About a year. Maybe a little more."

"You got it typed up yet?"

"Almost. I have this odd little pastime I pursue that's called a job, Tyler. You remember? Edward Bear, friendly checker at your local Safeway Market? I have to pay rent, buy gas, eat, stuff like that. Luxuries."

"I do that," he said.

"I know, but the government pays you. That Uncle Sam you're always complaining about. Sends you a check every month. *Here, Tyler, here's some money.*"

"I earned that money," he said.

"And now you're on the dole."

"On the dole…Sounds like something out of the thirties. You make it sound like I'm doing something wrong. I paid into that system for years. Now it's my turn."

"For years," I said. "Didn't you tell me you spent some of those long, fruitful, taxpaying years locked up in the slammer?"

"...A few."

"Like two? Three?"

"Couldn't have been more than five...six at the outside. Plus a little county jail time."

"Long time," I said.

"You really had to be there to appreciate it."

"What I mean is that us law-abiding taxpayers were supporting you all those years when you were lounging around in prison making license plates or burlap sacks. Or whatever you did in there...You know somebody told me it costs just as much to keep a man in prison for a year as it does to send him to Harvard."

"Or a woman."

"You know what I mean."

"I do. And it does. Just different kinds of education. Institutions of higher and lower learning. It's not always clear which is best. And though prisons don't give out diplomas, there are certificates that indicate you have completed the curriculum. There's one that's called a Parole, which confirms the fact that you have completed the course and are being released with certain restrictions, though perhaps only temporarily."

"And you have some of those certificates." It was not quite a question.

"I do...But we digress. *The Seven Deadly Needs.* Almost finished?"

"Close. A few weeks and it's done."

"Good."

"...Why?" I can't help it; I'm suspicious by nature. And I know Tyler. Why would he be pleased that I was almost finished unless he had something else for me to do?

"Because we have another project, Edward."

Of course. I knew it.

"I knew that," I said.

"Doubtful," he remarked dryly.

"No, I actually did know. All these years, Tyler, and I can actually tell what you're thinking."

"I'm...transparent?"

"You're obvious at times."

"Ah, obvious," he said. "I like transparent better."

"So what do I do with *The Seven Deadly Needs* when I get finished?"

"Find a publisher."

"Sure. A publisher. Why didn't I think of that? You think you just call up and get a publisher? *Hello, Doubleday? This is unknown author Edward Bear, calling to let you know that we're going to let you publish our next book. Yes, the usual six figure advance will be fine.* Jeez, Tyler."

"Confidence, lad," he said. "Confidence. Believe and all things are possible. Besides, you're the writer. You're supposed to know about these kind of things."

"I've been writing for ten years, Tyler. Ten years...and I haven't had one word published. Not one. You know how many publishers, how many editors and associate editors and just plain flunkies I've contacted in those ten years?"

"Four million."

"Five hundred and something by latest count. I keep track. I've averaged about one a week for ten years. Fifty contacts, fifty rejections every year. Perfect balance. For ten years. Ten, Tyler. I have a filing cabinet drawer full of rejection slips."

"Well, when you get to be an overnight success you can point to all your hard work, grit and determination. Good American qualities. Everybody loves hard work, grit and determination. You can go on Oprah and be a symbol of

America's underclass who has risen above tragic circumstances to achieve wealth and fame beyond your wildest dreams. I can see the headlines: *Misunderstood Writer Achieves Fame & Fortune.* Throw in a few tidbits about recovery and you're a guaranteed folk hero."

"Tyler, Tyler..."

"I love you, Edward. Try to remember that."

"Ahhh..." He is sometimes at his most exasperating when he is being kind and understanding. I never know how to respond. "I think I like it better when you adopt your slightly more cynical role. You're so...conciliatory sometimes. I never know how to deal with that."

"Me? I'm easy. I'm an open book. Transparent you said?"

"I believe I said obvious."

"You think I'm being deliberately evasive? Ambiguous perhaps."

"I think that's a definite possibility," I said.

"Well, the one thing I don't want to do is be predictable. I couldn't stand that, and neither could you...And you might want to consider the possibility that all this could be a part of your ongoing education."

"I'll...consider that," I said.

"Just think, you could even become famous like...who was the guy who wrote the biography of Samuel Johnson?"

"Boswell. James Boswell. You're suggesting I could be the Edward Bear to your Tyler."

"Something like that."

"Other than the fact that Tyler's not your real name and Edward Bear's not mine, it's a perfect fit."

"So who cares?" said Tyler. "What's in a name..."

"I know...A rose by any other name..."

"Well said."

"So, Maestro, what's this other project you have in mind?"

"It's not obvious?"

"Well…"

"You mean given enough time you could come up with the answer."

"I could," I said.

"I'll save you the extra labor. Man in my position wants to save time. Needs to save time."

"Last few innings and all that."

"Right. The next project is *The Seven Deadly Fears*."

"Ah," I said. "*The Seven Deadly Fears*."

"See, you've already got a handle on it."

"Not quite."

"It's simple," he said.

"No. My guess is that it's not simple at all. That's the phrase you use when something is actually very complex and you want me to feel bad because I don't understand it."

"First of all, I never want you to feel bad, Edward. Ever. But if, in the process of receiving information, or instruction, you allow yourself to feel bad, that's a pumpkin of a different color. You might possibly take comfort in the fact that there is never any malice intended."

"…Possibly," I said.

"You remember *The Seven Deadly Needs*?"

"Who could forget? A landmark work…which may someday even get published."

"Which *will* get published."

"Okay, will get published."

"And be a big success."

"I thought you didn't care about any of that."

"I don't," he said. "That's why it's going to be a big success…Anyway, it's like that; like *The Seven Deadly Needs*. You remember. We tape-recorded the conversations and you typed them up. *Are* typing them up. Only now we have *Fears* instead of *Needs*. And we talk about them. Discuss them. Like we did."

"So we're going to do a whole book about fears?"

"That's the plan. Realizing, of course, that some fears are normal. Some are even healthy. Necessary. We're not interested in those."

"Like my fear of Maynard Jenson when I was in the fourth grade."

"Probably a very rational fear. Maynard was…?"

"A bully who liked to punch people in the face. Me especially."

"Well then Maynard would be considered a very rational fear," he said. "It's the pathological fears I'm referring to. The ones that keep us from enjoying life. The ones that block the sunlight of the spirit."

"Like for instance…?"

"Well, if I was afraid of heights, maybe I could never get on an airplane and be able to travel. Or climb a mountain. If I was afraid of, I mean really terrified of, intimacy, which is actually one of the fears I'm thinking about, maybe I could never have a decent relationship. And of course the opposite of fear is…what?"

"…Faith?"

"Well done, Star Pupil."

"Faith in what? You're not going to pull one of those mumbo jumbo routines about the Great Pumpkin, are you?"

"What's mumbo jumbo about the Great Pumpkin?" said Tyler. "I love the Great Pumpkin."

"I know you do, but it's very…comic strippy."

"Comic strippy?"

"Yeah…comic strippy. You know."

"It's just that I don't want us to get into the Heavy Does It business, Edward, where voices tend to get an octave

7

lower and everybody gets Ve-ry Serious and we talk about Gawd. I thought maybe we could talk about trust, or the process, or how we might rely on the Community to help us deal with fears. Or even the Great Pumpkin. Maybe dance a bit. Sing. That sometimes helps. Irreverence has always seemed like a safer path. And actually much more spiritual."

"You think?"

"I do. Now the first thing we do is try to make them visible. The fears. And sometimes just acknowledging them goes a long way toward resolving them. Father Keating says that emotions are energy and often the only way to dissipate the energy of troubling emotions is to acknowledge and articulate them. I think that's almost word for word. Then, of course, action follows."

"Of course. And Father Keating is…?"

"A Trappist monk," he said. "And writer. One of the good guys."

"And you know him?"

"I've met him a few times."

"My Mentor with the Dark Side has been out traveling in some very lofty spiritual company."

"I take an occasional trip to the home of the spiritual elite. A day trip. I'm not to be mistaken for one of them. "

"Hardly a danger, Maestro. Believe me. So you've got a list of fears?"

"I'm working on it," he said. "Getting lists from every-body. I have dozens of fears. Any ideas?"

"Lots."

"Like what?"

"Like…Fear of death, fear of change. I ever tell you I was afraid of the dark."

"No."

"Still," I said.

"What do you do about it?"

"First thing is I never tell people about it."

"Until now," he said.

"Right. And I have no idea why I told you. What I do about it is I go down in the basement, turn off all the lights and sit in the dark."

"That help?"

"…Maybe," I said. "Mostly I can't really tell. I know I'm terrified every time I do it."

"Talking about it helps…You ever meet anyone else who was afraid of the dark?"

"Not any grownups. I mean it's not something that comes up in casual conversation."

"I'll bet there's lots of people who are afraid of the dark."

"Grownups?"

"Yeah, grownups," he said. "You may even start to meet some now."

"Why now?"

"Just happens that way sometimes. I mean once you recognize it and say it out loud things begin to happen. We'll log it under Fear of the Unknown."

"And talking about it helps?"

"It does. The one thing we do know is that *not* talking about it *doesn't* help. I'm as sick as my secrets. You remember. So we'll talk. Share experience, strength and hope."

"Film at eleven," I said.

"Get the tape recorder warmed up. I'll be at your place next Tuesday. Seven sharp."

"I'll be ready."

"I know you will. You're an absolute wonder."

"…Is that a compliment?"

"It is," said Tyler.

"Did the Rockies win today?"

"They were playing the Braves, Edward."

9

"So?"

"The Rockies don't win when they play the Braves," he said.

"Oh...See you Tuesday."

"You shall indeed."

CHAPTER 1

FEAR OF THE UNKNOWN

"You must do the thing you think you cannot do."
                                    Eleanor Roosevelt

"The only thing we have to fear is fear itself."
                                    FDR

I don't know why, but when we first get together before we start these long dialogues, it always seems awkward. It's almost like we have to sneak up on the topic. Or maybe each other. Weird. I mean we've known each other for a long time, spent hours together talking about everything you can think of, but it still seems weird. Maybe it's because we get into new territory every time it happens. And there's something about him that defies description, some...quality maybe that I don't have a name for. What I know is that whenever I'm with him, I just feel better.

So I got him his cup of coffee, which he absolutely has to have before he can do anything, even talk, then found an ashtray so he could indulge his nicotine habit. Even had to dig up the matches. I told him that all he has are a lot of bad habits and that it's absolutely unconscionable that he still smokes. But it's no fun getting on his case because he just shakes his head and agrees. I offered an opening.

"I made out a list of fears, too," I said,

"Good. Always use more lists."

"You want to start with my list?"

"No," he said.

"Why? You don't think my list is any good?"

"How would I know if your list is any good? I haven't even seen it. It might be a terrific list."

"Then why don't we use it?"

"…Because we're going to use mine."

"Jeez," I said.

"Jeez what?" he said. "What?"

"I mean here I am offering to help with the list and you just…trash my offer."

"I didn't trash your offer, Edward. I just said it would be better if we used my list. Direct and to the point. No trashing involved."

"It's a control issue."

"No, it's not a control issue."

"Can I do the fear for next week?"

He didn't say anything for a few seconds.

"Sure," he said finally. "We probably have lots of the same fears listed anyway."

"Like what?"

"For one thing, fear of the unknown."

"That include fear of the dark?"

"It does."

"That's on my list, too, fear of the dark," I said.

"I know. I just listed it under fear of the unknown. For convenience. So why are you afraid of the dark?"

"I don't think I know."

"Dig a little."

"The dark seems...threatening somehow. Spooky. I mean there's lots of things going on in the dark that you can't see."

"And you don't think they could be good things?" he said.

"Not a chance."

"You've always been afraid?"

"Ever since I can remember," I said.

"Are you afraid when you just close your eyes? I mean if the lights were on in the room and you closed your eyes, would you be afraid?"

"...I don't think so."

"Try it," said Tyler. "Close your eyes."

I closed my eyes.

"Is it dark?"

"Yeah."

"You afraid?" he said.

"Not really."

"Why not?"

"Because...For one thing I know the lights are actually on; all I have to do is open my eyes and look around. I mean if anything got too close, I could open my eyes and see it. Plus, you're here. So I'm not really alone."

"So maybe you're afraid of being alone."

"I'm not afraid of being alone when the lights are on."

"What if the lights were off and I was here."

"I'd be...less afraid."

"Why?" he said.

"Because...if there was something there, in the dark, you could maybe help me."

"Help you what?"

"...Protect me."

"From what?"

"I don't know from what, Tyler. If I knew from what it wouldn't be fear of the unknown, would it?"

"Good point," he said. "So basically you're afraid of the unknown and the darkness just magnifies the fear."

"You want me to say that?" I said.

"I want you to say whatever you feel."

I only partially believe that. Most times I think he just wants me to agree with him.

"You ever get locked in a closet when you were little?" I said.

"I did. I come from a long line of alpha males who thought that those kinds of experiences made men out of boys."

"Me, too. I spent a lot of time in closets."

"That why you're afraid of the dark?" he said.

"Maybe. I remember that I always wanted to sleep with the light on in my room."

"You're in good company. I understand that Gandhi was afraid of the dark and always kept a light burning by his bed."

"Really?"

"That's what they say."

"...Man."

"And I bet your father told you that only sissies slept with the light on."

"How did you know that?"

"We had the same father," he said. "Same type. A generation apart but the same guy...What did you think being a sissy meant?"

"I wasn't sure," I said. "I just knew by the way he said it that I didn't want to be one."

"Did you think it meant being like a girl?" he said.

"A girl or...maybe a coward."

"Something you didn't want to be."

14

"Right," I said. "I mean when you're seven or eight, girls are the most useless things on the face of the earth. You know that."

"Just think, the worst thing he could say about you was that you were acting like a girl. And we wonder why we have such conflicted ideas about women...You wet the bed when you were a kid?" he said.

"You been talking to my therapist?"

"You don't have a therapist, Edward. I happen to know that because sons of alpha males don't seek out therapists or counselors, usually not even medical doctors because we don't....we don't what, Edward?"

"Don't want to be considered sissies?"

"Bravo, Star Pupil. Mainly because we know that only sissies ask for help. We know that. We are actually born with that knowledge. It's like a basic instinct, like bees knowing where to find honey. That's why it's so amazing that any of us get into recovery. We prefer death or at the least excruciating pain to asking for help."

"And this has what to do with the fear of the dark?"

"Everything. Stay tuned. So you eventually learned to sleep with the light off?"

"Let's say I learned to sleep with less light."

"And stopped wetting the bed?"

"Eventually. They gave me something called Tofranil."

"It helped?"

"Must have. I know I got a little buzz off it. I also got the brandy and eggnog treatment because I was a skinny little kid and that was supposed to help me gain weight."

"Lucky you," he said. "I was a fat little kid. Believe me skinny is better. And look at the up side. You got an early start on those drug and alcohol problems. Ahead of the pack, so to speak."

"Practice, practice, practice. So here I was eight or nine years old and I couldn't go anywhere overnight because of The Problem. Actually *we* couldn't go anywhere overnight; that's what drove them crazy. *We'd love to come over, Aunt Emma, but my defective son will pee all over your couch if we do.* I don't think he actually ever said that, since the subject was strictly taboo, but I'm sure that's what he was thinking. We, in fact, were not allowed to talk about it. At all. Though my sister managed some snide comments from time to time."

"You ever call her a sissy? Your sister?"

"Had absolutely no effect," I said. "She was older. And tougher. She got smacked around because she wasn't a boy, and I got smacked around because, although I actually was a boy, I wasn't the right kind, the tough kind."

"The prototype of the American Family. You're the wrong thing, or even if you are the right thing, you're not enough of the right thing to really count."

"They were desperate. Especially my father. I think he felt that my peeing in the bed every night reflected poorly on him. My mother tried waking me up every two hours to go to the bathroom. She even prayed about it. St. Jude, Patron Saint of Hopeless Causes. Very religious woman. *Dear St. Jude, please help my son to stop peeing in the bed.*"

"No help?" he said.

"None," I said. "My father felt that I wasn't really trying. Not really. It was incomprehensible to him that I couldn't stop. He thought I was doing it on purpose."

"Nothing like waking up in a cold damp bed to make you feel good in the morning," said Tyler. "I personally loved it. The smell of stale urine, the cold sheets. Man, nothing like it. Matter of fact, I liked it so much I started doing it again when I got older, when ingesting large quantities of alcohol and various drugs had become my main

16

purpose in life. So what did they do to get you straightened out."

"The Tofranil actually seemed to work."

"A cocktail for the lad," he said. "Tofranil and brandy and eggnog."

"Yeah."

"And sleeping with the light on? "

"Eventually we got down to one of those little night-lights. Only slightly better than nothing. I stole a flashlight and read under the covers at night. Had to steal the batteries, too, but it was worth it. I was heavily into adventure stories —Treasure Island, Moby Dick, Tarzan, all those Zane Grey books. I'm sure my mother knew, but she never told Dad."

"Your first escape—books. So, after a somewhat traumatic beginning, you grew up to be happy and well-adjusted."

"Tyler, you know my story. You know that's not true. One bad decision after another, eventually leading to the Bottom of the Barrel and thence to recovery. I didn't display good judgment about anything. A very ugly picture."

"Would it surprise you to know that this fear-of-the-unknown, fear-of-the-dark thing we've been talking about was related to other fears?"

When he poses a question like that I never answer right away. Even if I think I know the answer. Sometimes the question is not as straightforward as it appears, and some-times it's actually a trap. And, yes, Tyler is capable of that.

"...I may have known that. Suspected it at least."

"You see," he said, "you grew up in an atmosphere where fear was not an acceptable emotion. Fear of anything. So did I. Some of us learned to deal with it by just denying it. *What, me afraid? No way. I will now do something so foolhardy and life-threatening that you will not believe there is an ounce of fear anywhere in my body.* You ever do that?"

17

"I have."

"Some turned it into anger and made the transition so quickly they never knew they were afraid. They were just angry all the time and didn't know why. Others managed to learn more acceptable ways of dealing with it and expressing it. I didn't."

"How did you deal with it?"

"I did the anger thing. My father would've been proud of me, but the whiskey got to his liver before I really got a handle on it, so he wasn't around to see the results of all that training."

"...You need more coffee?"

He tilted his cup and looked into it.

"Not yet," he said. "Now if you have what I often refer to as a Broken Brain, and I believe we share that particular affliction, when something happens, some random event, the brain automatically goes to the Worst Case Scenario. Without hesitation. It's almost like it's pre-programmed. Every headache is brain cancer. Every rejection is complete and total abandonment. All criticism is ridicule. Suicide seems like the proper response to a flat tire. Broken Brains are not well suited to moderate solutions."

"I can believe that."

"So when you're in-the-dark, or afraid of the dark, or the unknown, the Broken Brain goes immediately to the Worst Case Scenario and plays it out like a movie in your head."

"And why, Old Wise One, does it do that? Or better yet, why is it broken?"

"I'm not sure. Sometimes I think of it as a Manufacturing Defect and sometimes I think it may have been damaged through improper use. You know, constantly inputting the wrong messages, excessive use of drug therapy, stress fractures at the edges of reality, some sort of trauma, maybe genetics, lots of possibilities. Truth of it is, I don't really know."

"There's no use being old, Tyler, if you can't at least be smart."

"Is the dark filled with terrible things?" he said, as if he had not heard my comment.

"Yeah."

"Like what?"

"...Spiders, for one thing," I said.

"Ah, spiders..."

"Big spiders."

"Why?"

"Why spiders?"

"Yeah, why spiders?"

"The closet," I said. "I got locked in the closet when I wet the bed. And I always thought there were spiders in the closet. Tarantulas...You ever see a tarantula?"

"Just pictures."

"Doesn't do them justice. Seemed like they were all over the farm when I was a kid. My father used to kill them with the flat side of a scoop shovel. *Wham!* I was always afraid they were going to jump twenty or thirty feet and land on my face. Kind of a revenge thing against my father. Like, *Since we can't get to the big guy with the shovel, let's take out the kid.*"

"You ever find a tarantula in the closet?"

"...No."

"Tell me what happens when you go down to your basement and turn the lights off."

"Panic. I can't breath."

"Are there spiders?"

"Sometimes. Worse yet, there are these...things. Ominous, threatening things moving in my direction."

"What happens when they get real close?"

"I turn the lights on."

"And the things?"

"Gone."

"Where?" he said.

"Maybe they live in the dark and they vanish when the lights come on."

"You believe that?"

"No," I said.

"What *do* you believe?"

"About the dark? What's in it?"

"Yeah," he said. "Besides the spiders."

"If I said demons, would you know what I meant?"

"I'd have a pretty good idea."

"That's what's in the dark," I said. "Demons."

"You ever think of making friends with the demons?"

"Tyler, Tyler…Sometimes I wonder about you."

"I have a story for you. This one is about Milarepa, the great Tibetan sage. You've heard of Milarepa?"

"From you."

"Milarepa was a holy man who lived in a cave high in the Himalayas. One day the demons came to the mouth of his cave howling and wailing, making all sorts of horrible noises, holding human skulls in their hands, blood dripping from their fingers. Milarepa looked up from his meditation and said, *Oh, come in, friends. You look tired. Please come in and have some tea.* So the demons came in, sat around the fire with Milarepa, had some tea, then curled up and went to sleep."

"And the moral of this high-minded tale?" I said.

"Make friends with your demons."

"What happens when the demons wake up, Maestro?"

"The process repeats. You make friends again. And again."

"Until…?"

"Until there are no more demons, only visitors to the cave. Friends."

"Ah…" I said, as if it made sense. "Only friends. And the demons are…I mean the demons represent the dark? The unknown?"

"The fear."

"And just how do I make friends with the dark?"

"Like Milarepa, you welcome it, welcome the unknown into your life. You stop fighting it. Stop running away. You embrace it. Think surrender. Think trust. And you learn to trust by trusting, if that happened to be your next question. Which is also how you learn to surrender."

"Fat chance."

"Start small; bigger things will follow."

"You ready for more coffee?"

"No. I have to go, my friend."

"Tyler, where can you possibly have to go? You don't work, you're not married, and as far as I know you don't have a sweetie hidden in a cave somewhere who dispenses sexual favors to senior citizens…Although didn't you tell me something about a woman you used to see? What was her name? Margaret? Margot? Do I remember you telling me that?"

"It seems unfortunate that I may have mentioned her. And her name is Mercedes."

"Like the car?"

"Exactly," he said.

"And she's a healer? A witch?"

"A *curandera*. A teacher. You could call her a medicine woman, but there's no real translation."

"Heavy. But she's not what you could call a sweetie?"

"No."

"So what do you do, you and Mercedes? You cast spells on people? Turn them into trees? Fire hydrants? Heal the sick? What?"

"We talk mostly. About life, other dimensions. She taught me things. Teaches me things."

"You still see her?"

"From time to time."

"She's old? Really old?"

"Ancient possibly," said Tyler.

"Older than you?"

"Yes."

"That's close enough to ancient for me...But if you're not going to see Mercedes, where could you possibly be going?"

"Into the night, Noble Student. Into the darkness. Where you should be going."

"Into the basement?"

"Into that treasure trove of inky blackness where there are lessons to be learned, demons to befriend. Remember the sequence—acknowledge, articulate...and the third part, Edward?

"After the acknowledge and articulate?"

"The third and perhaps most important part."

"When did we talk about it?"

"Last week," he said.

"Give me a hint."

"...Starts with *A*."

"Knowing you, it must be action."

"Bingo," said Tyler.

"I'll make a start. I'll embrace the darkness..."

"Good. And think about next week."

"I have. And you know what? I don't really want to pick the next fear. I want you to."

"You honor me by allowing me to choose."

22

"I'm not sure I want to go that far."

"It's too late," he said. "I'm already feeling honored."

"Just my luck. You want to give me a hint about what the fear is for next week?"

"I would, but I don't know yet."

"You're going to surprise me?" I said.

"Maybe both of us. Here's a little wisdom from Ralph Waldo Emerson—*Do the thing you fear and the death of fear is certain.*"

"Wise words."

"Ain't they, though…"

CHAPTER 2

FEAR OF CONFLICT, ANGER, CONFRONTATION

"Fear makes the wolf bigger than he is."
German proverb

"How was your week in the darkness?" he said.

"I'd call it an exercise in futility."

"You visited the basement often?"

"I did."

"And...?"

"I don't know if I can honestly say I was able to embrace the darkness, Tyler. Not like a warm cozy hug."

"I see," he said. "Well, you're only at the beginning. The road is long."

"If I know you, you more than likely have some borrowed words of wisdom to cover the situation."

"I do...How about, *In the game of life, nothing is less important than the score at halftime.*"

"Jimmy the Greek?"

"I don't think so. The Greek would have had some odds on the halftime score. It was most likely some anonymous troll with a strange sense of humor."

"Man...I've been thinking, why are we doing this?"

"Taping all this? Writing the book?"

"Yeah," I said. "Why?"

"It is, hopefully, instructional, Edward. Perhaps people will read and respond to it. You know, think about things in a different way. Maybe make a difference in somebody's life. If only one person gets it, we've done our job. You like books?"

"Yeah."

"Why?"

"Because...I love to read."

"Why?"

"Why, why, why. You know, you can be a real load with all this why stuff, Tyler."

"I know," he said, smiling. "And I can't tell you how much that pleases me."

"I think that's...perverse."

"Perhaps. But if we don't ask the questions, we never get to any of the answers. You know what the Greeks said about *The unexamined life*."

"That's Plato, right? The original why guy."

"Indeed," said Tyler. "Even before my time."

"Very old," I said. "The whole thing is something like, *The unexamined life is hardly worth living*."

"Close," he said.

"And you know what happened to Plato."

"That was Socrates they did away with."

"Whoever," I said. "He got the gas."

"The hemlock," he said.

"Same deal."

25

"Meaning?"

"Meaning they did him in."

"Why?"

"Because, Maestro, because he was always asking why, that's why. Even I remember that. You might want to take some time and think about that."

"You're not thinking of slipping me a little hemlock in my coffee, are you?"

"Nothing so drastic," I said. "At least not yet. And what does all this have to do with fear?"

"Consider the possibility that we might be afraid to take a good look at our lives. Afraid to examine them. All of us. Because once we do, we might actually have to make some changes. Take action. Scary thought."

"So all this is a segue into the fear for this week? The fear of change?"

"Actually, no," he said. "That's for later. This week it's the fear of conflict, confrontation, the fear of anger and its consequences."

"Hey, that's right up my alley. I majored in conflict and anger. And violence. I've even got the scars to prove it. I did graduate work right in my own home. Night school mostly, though there were some daytime courses."

"As I recall," said Tyler, "your formative years were spent in some significant degree of turmoil. Threats, intimidation, wars and rumors of wars, the whole gamut of physical and emotional trauma."

"True. I have less than fond memories of those years. I remember my father throwing my mother around. My mother throwing my sister around, and she, of course, throwing me around. Unfortunately, I was the youngest so I didn't get to throw anybody around. It was useless to try and fight back; my sister was a lot bigger and tougher than I was. Even the dog was bigger than I was. And besides always

26

smelling bad, he bit people. Defenseless souls like yours truly. Prince, the Family Dog. The Prince of Farts, I called him. That's when fart was a really bad word."

"It's not now?" said Tyler.

"See? You're so old you think that fart might still be a bad word. That's old. Fuck is not even a bad word anymore. People in polite society use it all the time."

"Guess I don't spend enough time in polite society."

"I've been telling you that for years. And remind me to take out this part when I type it up."

"Why?"

"Because that particular word doesn't fit in with the kind of book we're doing. Aren't we discussing fears, dilemmas, and solutions of a possibly spiritual nature? The same thing we did in *The Seven Deadly Needs?*"

"We are," he said.

"Well...Do I have to say more? I mean isn't it obvious?"

"Just leave it in for now. We can always take it out later. I don't want to start editing the conversation to make it sound good. Or worse yet make it sound like we changed it to protect the innocent."

"I vote we take it out," I said.

"Your vote is duly noted."

"But won't count."

"...Might. You ever read that book—*Conversations With God?*"

"Yeah."

"You think that guy was really talking to God?"

"No."

"Neither did I," he said. "I figure either everybody talks to God or nobody does. I don't want this to appear like we edited it as we went along and just left in the stuff that sounded good."

"You think he did that? The guy who wrote *Conversations*?"

"I think maybe. Sounds too perfect. I think it's possible that God may actually use bad grammar. And an occasional four letter word. I mean if it was called for. If it was necessary to get someone's attention."

"You mean a four letter word other than love."

"Exactly."

"Wouldn't *that* be a revelation. But what I'm trying to get at, Tyler, is that you'll never get an editor to agree with you. The kind of places that publish the stuff you write, don't publish stuff that has words like that in it. No way. You're just making it hard on yourself."

"I'll take the chance," he said.

"Of course, and then blame me because I can't find a publisher...But we're wasting time, Maestro; lets get back to the fear of anger, conflict, et cetera."

"So what was your house like? Your growing-up house."

"Well, you know a little about it, the People Throwing Contests and all that. If I could have just had somebody to throw around I probably would have been alright. At least I would have felt better. I actually prayed for a little brother just so I wouldn't be the bottom of the food chain. Even a little sister and, believe me, that was desperation."

"Amen," he said. "You afraid of anger today? Conflict?"

"Yeah," I said.

"Why?"

"It's not safe."

"How is it not safe?" said Tyler.

"I had this deal figured out early on. When somebody got angry, somebody got hurt. It was like a House Rule. It was the very first connect-the-dots emotional puzzle that I figured out. Anger equals pain and suffering, usually mine."

"It's the domino theory—Conflict to Anger to Confrontation to Violence, they just tumble right into each other. So what did you do?"

"What-did-I-do?...You know I never thought much about what I actually did. You know, how I coped with it."

"That's why we're doing it now; trying to find out."

"Will it make a difference?" I said.

"Maybe."

"That's what I like about you, Tyler. You're always so definite about things. What does *maybe* mean?"

"It means we're going to have to *do* it, talk about it and go through what you may think of as a useless exercise and see if it makes a difference. Life is Learn-By-Doing, Edward. You know that. Not Learn-By-Thinking, which is what you intellectual types would prefer."

"Who cares what I did or how I did it? I survived, that's what I did. I didn't know it wasn't normal. I never asked other kids if they got locked in the closet, or if their fathers shot .22 caliber bullets up through the ceiling when they were sleeping upstairs."

"It matters, Noble Student, because you might still be repeating old survival skills that inhibit your journey along life's glorious highway."

"Ah," I said. "Life's glorious highway. Of course."

"So, your coping skills consisted of...?"

"Let me think...I tried to stay out of the way. I remember that. Spent lots of time hiding. I spent a lot of time climbing the big eucalyptus tree in the back yard. Way up high. I figured if I didn't say anything or do anything too obvious, they would forget I was there. That was one thing. My sister, who was much more visible, took a lot of the heat. She had a weight problem. My mother, who must have come in a good deal over two bills, encouraged her to eat. *Want some more, Sally, honey? Have another scoop of mashed potatoes."*

"Armor," he said. "To cover up the fear?"

"Possibly."

"And you?"

"I was doing eggnog and brandy and wetting the bed on a regular basis. Embarrassing my father."

"So what do you do today when you're around conflict? How do you deal with it?"

"I...run from it. I get away somehow. On rare occasions I have been known to attack rather than run, which I understand is not a good response. At least I don't drink or take drugs anymore. But you know I can't even be around people who are arguing. Even if it's just on the radio. It makes me so uncomfortable, I have to change the station."

"Is that okay?" he said.

"I don't know if it's okay, Tyler. It's what I do."

"Think about this. If you're three years old and your mother tells you not to cross the street alone, that's good advice. If you're thirty and you're still afraid to cross the street, that may be a problem."

"You're suggesting that this person doesn't know why he's afraid to cross the street?"

"Something like that."

"And you think there may be things in my life that are equivalent to being afraid to cross the street. Hidden, perhaps, in some dark cellar in my mind."

"Ah, you writers," he said. "You have such a way with words."

"And just how would I go about finding out if that was true? The thing about not being able to cross the street."

"Oh, I thought you'd never ask."

"No, you didn't," I said. "You don't fool me for a minute, Tyler. You maneuvered the whole thing around so

30

that I'd actually be forced to ask. You forget that I know you so well."

"I'm humbled by your insight," he said.

"I bet."

"But now that you ask, I'll tell you. Inform you. Of course all this assumes that you've already done a regular fourth step inventory."

"Tyler, people who aren't in recovery aren't going to know what a fourth step inventory is."

"...Good point," he said. "So they can just skip the fourth step part and go on."

"Simple...but confusing."

"It's the best I can do on short notice. So you find out about lots of that hidden stuff by doing a Belief Inventory. About the fear of anger and conflict in this case. And violence."

"Naturally," I said. "A Belief Inventory. Can't imagine why I didn't think of that."

"And how, you ask, how do you do a Belief Inventory?"

"I'm asking that?"

"You are."

"Okay. How do you do a Belief Inventory?...Why is it that I feel like I'm the straight man in some bad Abbott and Costello movie?"

"In substance, here's what you do. You get a piece of paper..."

"Lined paper? Notebook paper? Typing paper?"

"Just paper, Edward. Any kind will do. Don't complicate the process. At the top of the page you write Belief Inventory."

"That's in case I forget what I'm doing?"

"No. That's so you'll know what it is when you pick it up a year from now. Under the Belief Inventory, you put what the belief is that you're going to inventory. In this case it happens to be about the fear of anger, conflict and so forth. But it can be about anything. Guilt. Religion. Relationships. Work. Sex…"

"Oh, boy."

"And we may actually touch on some of those when we get to the other fears. Anyway, it can be about anything. Then you draw a line down the center of the page."

"Top to bottom?"

"Either way. On the top of the left side you write Old Beliefs and on the top of the right side you write New Beliefs. Then under the Old Beliefs side you write down some old beliefs."

"Like, Sex is…sinful. And bad. Causes acne, dandruff, insanity…"

"We're not doing a sex inventory right now, Edward. Let's stick with the fear of anger and conflict. How about, When somebody gets angry, somebody gets hurt. That's an old belief you have, right?"

"Right."

"So you put that down on the old belief side and under the new belief side you put a belief that you're in the process of acquiring or that you'd *like* to acquire, some new belief that may be healthier than the old one."

"Like for instance?"

"Oh…Expressing anger is better than denying it. Conflict may be a positive force in problem resolution."

"Think about one for sex."

"A new belief one?" he said.

"Yeah."

"Sex is terrific. And good for you…You have trouble with sex?"

"Doesn't everybody?"

"Probably…But you get the picture? About belief inventories?"

"I think so," I said. "You write lots of old beliefs?"

"As many as you can come up with in twenty minutes. About that one subject."

"And how many new beliefs?"

"For every old belief you write a new one that will serve you better."

"What if I don't believe the new belief?"

"You just have to be *willing* to believe, Edward. It's a start. A goal to work toward."

"Willing. Got it. So how about, Sex is a wonderful expression of love?"

"That may work if you're doing an inventory about sex, Edward. It may not be as...appropriate for another kind of inventory."

"So when are we going to do the sex one?"

"As a matter of fact, next week we're doing the Fear of Intimacy."

"I'm not afraid of intimacy, Tyler. I've been married three times."

"And divorced three times."

"The American Way."

"Indeed," he said. "So now that you've spent your twenty minutes writing old and new beliefs, you take your pencil and you cross out each of the old beliefs and write FALSE in large letters through it."

"And that makes it go away?

"It's an action, Edward, that indicates your willingness to discard an old belief that no longer serves you well. You're telling the Universe that you're ready to get out of the problem and into the solution. You know, *Action is the magic word.*"

"I remember. So pretty soon I'll be able to cross the street?"

"Let's just say that your chances will be a lot better than they were."

"A lot better meaning sixty percent? Eighty percent?"

"I have to go, Edward. I feel a headache coming on."

"You should write about headaches, Maestro. What you believe causes them. All three of my ex-wives suffered from headaches."

"I can't imagine why," said Tyler.

"Me neither."

"So are we clear about the Belief Inventory?"

"We are. And I'm going to get started. Soon."

"Good. . ."

"And now you're off to the Laundromat?"

"Every Tuesday."

"You know, there's a book called *Tuesdays With Morrie*. You ever read it?"

"I have. Wonderful book."

"I wonder sometimes if we're meeting every Tuesday because you want this to be a book like *Tuesdays With Tyler.*"

"The Laundromat is open late on Tuesdays, Edward."

"Oh."

"I leave you with a thought from Eileen Caddy: *Thoughts are like boomerangs.*"

"Which actually means. . .?"

"That I'll see you next week."

". . .Good night."

CHAPTER 3

FEAR OF INTIMACY

"The course of true love never did run smooth."
William Shakespeare

"You know, that belief inventory thing is hard."

"How so?" said Tyler.

"When I started to write down my old beliefs about conflict and anger and all that stuff, when I really start to think about it, I don't know *what* I believe. Am I supposed to know? I mean do other people know?"

"Some do, some don't."

"How do I find out?"

"You want me to give you the answers, too, Edward?"

"No, I just want some help. Aren't you supposed to be helping me? I mean isn't that what we're supposed to be doing with all this tape recording and book writing? Aren't we supposed to be helping people find answers?"

"True."

"But I don't even understand the questions. Or maybe it's the process I don't understand. And I'm no dummy. Wouldn't you say that I'm at least reasonably intelligent?"

"I would say that. I would go so far as to say that you're brighter than most."

"And if I don't get it," I said, "what about the rest of the people?"

"I surrender. So what is it about your old beliefs that you find so mystifying?"

"You know the example that we used? When somebody gets angry, somebody gets hurt?"

"Yeah," he said.

"Well, that's *true*, Tyler. That's what happened."

"So?"

"I mean it happened."

"Wasn't it true that it was dangerous to cross the road when you were three years old?"

"Yeah."

"Does that mean it has to be true forever?"

"...No."

"So," said Tyler, "just because the statement was true at one time, doesn't mean it's always going to be true. You're not a victim. Don't forget that. You're not at the mercy of some tragic childhood event or series of events. Or some information you received that doesn't apply anymore. Unless you believe that you are. Then, of course, you are."

"And it doesn't make any difference if the old belief was true or false? That what you're saying?"

"Think of it simply as a belief that doesn't serve you well."

"How about an example."

"What if you believed that if you're poor you can't be happy?"

"I do believe that."

"Perfect. What would you like to believe?"

"I'd like to believe that...I could be happy whether I had money or not."

"And that's what you put under the new belief side of the inventory sheet."

"That I'll be as happy as the proverbial clam whether I'm dead broke or I have a million dollars?"

"Yeah. So with the new belief that you're trying to incorporate into your impoverished life, you'll be moving in a direction that will de-emphasize the importance of money as a prerequisite for happiness. It's progress, not perfection. I'm sure you've heard the phrase. We are not shooting for overnight changes."

"We're not?"

"No," said Tyler. "Patience, O Restless One. It takes time to unravel beliefs. Very powerful forces at work. You have enough information now to continue with your inventory on anger and conflict?"

"I think so. Tune in next week."

"Good. We can now proceed with the fear for this week."

"Which is?"

"The Fear of Intimacy."

"I don't think I have that one."

"Intimacy is characterized by emotional closeness."

"I was married three times," I said.

"I know that. Warmth, caring, affection—any of those ring a bell?"

"Doesn't being married three times indicate that I was capable of some form of intimacy?"

"No," said Tyler.

"No? I can't believe you said that."

"You want me to say it again?...No. That better?"

"Jeez, Tyler. You don't know how I was with those women. I was actually very intimate. I mean we did some very intimate things. You might even be shocked by some of the things we did. *I'm* shocked when I think about them. I bought their underwear, for chrissakes. What's more intimate than that?"

"I'm not talking about sex, Edward. I'm talking about the fear of being emotionally close. Open, as it were. Honest, self-revealing."

"You went to Catholic high school, right?"

"We're changing the subject?" said Tyler.

"We're making a point."

"Okay. The answer is, yes, I went to a Catholic high school…until they asked me to leave."

"Man, if they could see you now, eh? Out riding the range with all those spiritual heavyweights."

"Proceed, Edward."

"Anyway, I made a novena to get laid when I was in high school. Loyola High. The Jesuits. I had my eye on Mary Ellen Ramage."

"What brings this up?"

"I'm being self-revealing."

Tyler moved his chair slightly.

"Perhaps I shouldn't be sitting so close to you. I don't want to get burned when the bolt of lightning comes zipping through the ceiling."

"We were just learning about the nine First Fridays, how you were going to get to heaven no matter what if you went to communion on nine consecutive First Fridays. At least I think that was the deal. Though I think there was something about Saturdays, too. Any of that sound familiar?"

"The Virgin Mary and the Blue Army?"

"Something like that. You may have been a little more Catholic than I was."

"Different generations," said Tyler. "I grew up in a generation when parents supported the idea that as long as a teacher wore a Roman collar, or a nun's habit, they were automatically right. Plus, we were heavily into discipline. And fear."

"Anyway, that's where I learned about novenas. That if you said certain prayers for a certain number of days, God would find it very difficult to turn down whatever your request was."

"And you were requesting Miss Ramage?" said Tyler

"I was. And God didn't seem to have any trouble at all denying my request. I prayed really hard, too."

"Probably good practice," he said.

"I don't know. Mary Ellen ended up with some pimply basketball player who was absolutely nowhere."

"And you?"

"I spent a lot of time in the bathroom. You know."

"Right," he said. "Stick time."

"But it turned out okay."

"How so?"

"I saw her at the twenty year reunion. She looked like the Pillsbury Doughgirl."

"And you, of course, were slim and trim as a panatela."

"I probably could lose a few pounds. It's not a big secret. Thirty or forty maybe."

"Do I hear fifty?"

"I don't know what happened. I started out as such a skinny kid."

"Bad gene pool," said Tyler. "But we digress, Noble Student. We're drifting away from the Fear of Intimacy. How well did any of your wives really know you?"

"...I'm not sure how to answer that."

"Let me help," said Tyler. "Did they know that you were afraid of the dark? That anger and conflict and the threat of violence absolutely terrified you? That you were..."

"Those aren't the kinds of things you tell women, Tyler. Certainly not wives. Those aren't the kinds of things you tell anybody."

"You're telling me," he said.

"Well, that's different. You're supposed to be my mentor. Aren't you sworn to secrecy or something. Isn't it against some Code of Honor to reveal any of this."

"We're writing a book about it, Edward."

"I know, but nobody knows who I am, right? I mean I could be anybody."

"And perhaps you are."

"What does that mean?"

"Perhaps you're the model for the Great American Male Myth about being bulletproof and invulnerable. *Faster than a speeding bullet. Able to leap tall buildings in a...*"

"Tyler, women don't want to be around men who are afraid of things. They're considered wimps."

"You ever ask?" he said.

"About what?"

"Never mind...Fear of intimacy also has a component that says *Nobody Will Like Me If They Find Out What I'm Really Like.* So we don't tell people. I mean what we're really like. Don't tell them anything...hopes, fears, dreams, any of it. Even the good stuff. Especially women. We decide what they want and then become that. It's a little like playing tennis by yourself."

"Why especially women?"

"Because they have something we want, Edward, and we're afraid that if we let them know anything about us that we consider less than Superman quality, we won't get it."

"I used to write poetry when I was in high school," I said.

"Good example. You ever tell anyone?"

"You kidding?"

"I had a friend," said Tyler, "who said he felt like John Wayne on the outside and Shirley Temple on the inside."

"Bad combination."

"Maybe Mary Ellen would have loved it if she knew you wrote poetry."

"I doubt that."

"But of course you'll never know...Things like the Fear of Looking Bad, Fear of Not Measuring Up, all parts of the Fear of Intimacy. You ever worry that your slausen wasn't big enough?"

"My slausen? Didn't I hear that years ago on a Johnny Carson Show? And does that mean what I think it means?"

"Most likely."

"Well, Tyler, that about settles it. You are never going to get this thing into print. Nobody, but no-body is going to publish it with stuff like that in it. First you use this...word that you can't use in a family publication, and now you want to talk about body parts. I think maybe if we're lucky we can get Playboy to do it in installments. Maybe Hustler or Penthouse or one of those."

"You didn't answer the question," he said.

"...What was the question?"

"I asked you if you ever worried about whether your slausen was big enough?"

"You think we're going to sneak it by the censors if we use a different word?"

"The question, Edward. The question."

"The answer is...You want the truth?"

"Of course I want the truth. Why would I ask the question if I didn't want the truth?"

"The answer is…I was concerned. Somewhat concerned. But who would you ask about something like that? I mean in case you were concerned. Which I wasn't really, because…there was no reason to be. Worried. Or concerned, for that matter."

"Good question," he said. "You can't ask guys. They'll be sure there's something wrong if you even have to ask. And most would lie anyway."

"Slightly concerned at the most…"

"My hunch is that most of us were," he said. "Or are. But it really doesn't matter."

"What do you mean it doesn't matter? That's all you hear about when you're growing up. That it *does* matter. Then you go see movies like Deep Throat and you hope that the woman you're going out with has never seen it. And never will."

"You think women worry?"

"About what?"

"About size?"

"I do think that."

"Well, most don't," he said. "The vast majority don't."

"And you know this because you've taken a survey, Maestro? You know this for a fact or is it just one of those …things you pick out of thin air to support some arbitrary position you've taken? Perhaps something you got from those Spiritual Gunslingers you're out riding the range with."

"You have to understand that women have enough to do worrying about how *they* look. And don't think for a minute that they get away free. Every women's magazine in the country has a woman on the cover who is air-brush perfect. And there are dozens of women's magazines. Dozens. So you're a woman and you're walking by a magazine rack and all you see are women who don't look like you or any other women that you know. And you are now positive that your boobs are too small, your hips are too big, and that everybody can see your cellulite thighs from hundreds of yards away. Even when you've got your raincoat on."

"What's all this have to do with intimacy?"

"How can I be intimate if I can't really let anybody know what I'm like? If I can't be open? Even let her know what I look like? And if I can't tell her my fears and she can't tell me hers, we are doomed to have this relationship where everything is shadow and nothing is substance. What I'd really like to do is to create this image of myself, maybe a little like Superman or Captain Marvel or Wonder Woman if that's your deal, have someone fall in love with it and see how long I can sustain the fantasy without anyone finding out."

"Finding out that it's only an image?" I said. "A projection?"

"Of course. That way I'll always look terrific and I'll never have to take a chance on anyone knowing what I'm really like. I'll be the Master Puppeteer that no one will ever see. Or get to know."

"Because if they get to know you…?"

"The fear is that if they get to know me, if I'm open, if we actually get intimate, they'll find out what I have known all along…that I'm hardly a person they'd like to know, for that matter that anybody would like to know, and that basically I'm defective. Unlovable. Perhaps even unlikable …I knew a guy who used to say that he did the best opening act in history. Flowers, phone calls, dinners, the whole thing. Women loved it. Trouble is he couldn't keep it up. When the curtain went up on act two, and he was Just Plain Bill, the Plumber, the women wanted to know where the Other Guy was, the guy from act one. So he ended up doing a lot of act ones."

"You think he would've been better off being Just Plain Bill from the beginning?"

"Yes, but that would take an act of great courage. It says, *Here's what I am. I trust you enough to show you what I think is the Real Me. Warts and all.*"

"Warts?"

"A figure of speech, Edward."

"Suicide, Tyler. Absolute suicide. Picture this in the personal ads: *Here I am, Cinderella. I'm forty pounds on the far side of slim...*"

"Do I hear fifty?"

"*...Jeez...Fifty pounds on the far side of slim and I've got a putz that's the size and shape of a tiny tuna can. I'm insecure, somewhat obsessive-compulsive, drank to excess for many years, though now sober, but basically I'm a pretty nice guy and I'd really like to make your acquaintance for a possible long term relationship.*"

"Just right," said Tyler.

"Sure. You know how many responses that ad gets? Zero. None. No responses at all. Or maybe one response from some lunatic. An ad like that will ensure my continuing celibacy for months, maybe years."

"You know, I think you're probably more intimate with me than you were with any of your wives."

I gave him a fishy look.

"Intimacy doesn't necessarily have anything to do with sex, Edward," he said.

"Well, that's a relief."

"And what passes for intimacy in men is that phony punch on the shoulder, the lecherous wink, and the snide, *Getting any lately, Frank?* That's intimacy for us. Male bonding. That's about as far as most of us get."

"So what do we do about it, about this unwillingness, this fear of intimacy?"

"First, you have to admit there *is* a fear of intimacy. That's the first step. Are we that far yet?"

"We…yes, I can get to that."

"Next, we have to understand that intimacy doesn't necessarily have anything to do with sex, size, technique, whether you're shopping at Frederick's of Hollywood, or your ability to quote, unquote, satisfy your partner. We there?"

"We are following along, Maestro. The pace is slow, but we are there."

"The armor that we wear protects us but also separates and isolates. It is necessary to remove the armor. Risky business. Understand that it takes courage to challenge any of the fears we have. And courage is defined as acting in the face of fear, not being fear-less."

"So what if it fails? What if I get all gooey and emotionally honest and warm and nobody shows up at my door? What do you have left? What do *I* have left?"

"Fortunately, not much," said Tyler. "Until a lot of the old baggage is discarded and you're free."

"I'll be standing naked for all the world to see, me and my tuna can putz and my extra fifty pounds. Free."

"Yes," he said. "Free." He made it sound like a terrific deal. But then, that's Tyler.

"I'm not sure that's such a wonderful deal."

"Well, the thing is, Noble Student, you have to try it to find out. Thinking about it won't help. When you get tired of having only superficial, surface relationships, you may be ready to *do* something."

"What do you think Mercedes would say?"

"About all this?" he said.

"Yeah. She might have a little more insight. A different take. You know."

"She might say something like, *It's better to go barefoot than to wear shoes with holes in the soles.*"

"Terrific...And this lady is a whizbang teacher? A healer of some kind?"

"Takes awhile to get it—what she says. You have to listen very carefully. There's usually a message beyond the words."

"Tyler, you know the weirdest people."

"The real mystery about Mercedes is that just being around her can make you feel whole and unbroken. Sacred even. It's very strange."

"I think maybe she's cast a spell on you, Maestro. I'd be a little careful if I were you. You're liable to wake up as a frog someday. She makes less sense than you do sometimes. If that's possible...Can we count on next week's fear being any easier?"

"I don't think they get any easier."

"And what *is* the fear for next week?"

"I haven't decided yet. I'll ask for guidance."

"From God?" I said.

"Or the Great Pumpkin."

"You'll be having a conversation with God-The-Great-Pumpkin? A regular conversation? Like that guy who wrote that book you don't believe in?"

"Not exactly what you'd call a regular conversation," he said. "There are...intermediaries."

"I see," I said. "Like people, or statues...You remember the waving statue you talked about? How about one of those? Maybe clouds talk to you. Or animals. How about animals? Squirrels maybe? Gathering nuts. That seems appropriate."

"...It varies, Edward. People sometimes. Dreams... Trees."

"Ah...My mentor talks to trees."

"I listen mostly."

"So if you wanted to have a conversation with God or a tree or the Great Pumpkin, where would you guys meet? I mean you have a special place? A church maybe? An orchard?"

"Somewhere between Here and There. And capitalize the Here and There."

"Somewhere between Here and There, eh?"

"Give or take a little."

"Jeez...Maybe you've been spending too much time around Mercedes."

"You know she plays checkers with God. Mercedes does."

"Interesting...She ever win?"

"I don't know. She never tells me how it comes out. And the only way I know she's playing is that she gets real quiet and just stares off into space. Then, once in awhile she says, *Your move, God.* That's how I know she's playing."

"And you think it's checkers?"

"I do."

"Why not chess?"

"I like to think of God as a checkers person. Someone who favors a simpler game."

"Spending time with Mercedes may not be the best thing for you, Maestro. Why don't you let me fix you up with a legitimate senior citizen, maybe one with blue hair who is strong in the family values department."

Tyler gave me one of his looks.

"Oh, Edward, sometimes I wonder about you. Although ...although there are times when I actually do seem to see some progress, slow as it might be. In the meantime, treat yourself kindly. If you do, the Universe will notice and do the same."

"That true?"

"Action, lad. It's the boomerang thing—what goes around, comes around. Try it and see. That's the only way to find out."

CHAPTER 4

FEAR OF CHANGE

For us, the status quo can only be for today, never
tomorrow. Change we must; we cannot stand still.

Bill W.

The universe is change; life is what thinking makes
it.

Marcus Aurelius

"You know who said, *If you pray for change, better
start packing*?"

"Jesus?" I said.

"No, not Jesus. You remember anything in the Bible
where Jesus says, *Start packing*?"

"No, but then I'm not a big Bible reader. But if it wasn't
Jesus, it must have been Shakespeare. Turns out that almost
every familiar saying comes out of the Bible or Shakespeare.
Something like eighty percent."

"I think this was Caroline Myss," he said. "At least
that's where I heard it."

"Who's Caroline Myss?"

"She's a lady who does energy medicine."

"I won't ask...I mean about the energy medicine deal. She's probably one of those ethnobotonists or Kirlian photographer types with a bone in her nose and a gourd full of ostrich teeth that she uses to drive away evil spirits. As I recall, you're fond of those types."

"I prefer to think of it as being open to new information," said Tyler. "Change, as it were. You may not be familiar with the term."

"With change?"

"I believe that was it."

"I'm not afraid of change, Maestro. Remember me? I'm the guy who's been married three times. That sound like I'm afraid of change?"

"As I recall those women left you for, what shall we call it...greener pastures? Didn't you tell me that?"

"Well, it wasn't like they just left me. Just up and walked out the door. It was more of a mutual decision. We decided, together we decided, that it wasn't working out."

"I thought you said Margaret left you for the guy who owned that jewelry store. The midget. What was his name?"

"Spencer. And he wasn't a midget. Where'd you get that idea?"

"You told me," said Tyler.

"I told you he was a *mental* midget. Not a regular midget. Some sort of a borderline moron."

"Who owned a jewelry store?"

"Right. And Marge loved jewelry. It was a natural."

"And the other two?" he said.

"Elaine and Nancy?"

"Surely you haven't forgotten their names."

"I married my first wife, the lovely and talented Nancy Cranebarger, when I was young," I said. "Very young. She was considerably older. What did I know? I was a babe in the woods."

50

"I have trouble picturing you as a babe in the woods."

"How smart could I have been at nineteen?"

"That's not a real question, is it?" said Tyler.

"...No."

"Because if it was, the answer would probably be, Not very."

"See? That's why I didn't make it a real question."

"And the lovely and talented Elaine?"

"Not to be critical, but it turned out that she was badly damaged. I mean even before we got married. Just a fact, Tyler, not a criticism. I found out later that she'd been living in some kind of mysterious...commune where they did some very strange things."

"For instance..."

"She was never too specific, but I was led to believe it had to do with some kind of weird sex thing."

"That's it?" said Tyler. "A weird sex thing?"

"That and a religious ceremony."

"She actually say it was weird?"

"...No. She just said it was a sex thing. And a religious thing."

"Lotta things," said Tyler.

"Better believe it."

"So she just start talking about it one day?"

"We were three years into it, into the marriage, which wasn't going all that well anyway, before she said a word about it. One day she just seemed to snap. Got very far out and started talking about it."

"You were still drinking then?"

"I was."

"And some of your behavior could have been a trigger event?"

"Well...She accused me of having an affair."

"True?"

51

"It wasn't really an affair, Tyler. It was more like a…"

"Never mind. I get the picture. So how long did…"

"Don't you want to hear about it?"

"No," he said.

"It wasn't like I did something terrible. All I did was…"

"You'll notice I'm ignoring your explanations."

"I am noticing," I said.

"So how long did your longest marriage last? What's the record?"

Tyler can be very stubborn at times.

"Okay, you win. My longest marriage was actually with Elaine. Before it began to unravel with the pills, the white port wine, reading the Bible out loud in the middle of the night, speaking in tongues. Yelling, actually. Started doing some other strange, self-destructive things."

"Like what?"

"She'd burn herself. You know, she'd hold a cigarette to her thigh till it burned a hole in it. I mean right in her skin. She had these…round burn marks all over her body. Very scary stuff."

"You divorced her?"

"She ran off with some guy had long hair and a beard. Drove a big truck. I sometimes picture both of them in the cab of that eighteen wheeler, rolling through the night at ninety miles an hour, popping pills, reading the Bible and yelling at Satan. Man…"

"So, basically, they all left you," said Tyler. "That a fair statement?"

"It wasn't like I didn't want them to go. I mean I was ready to have them go when they went. Believe me."

"But you didn't leave them?"

"What are you getting at? We're doing semantics here, Tyler. What difference does it make? We were ready to part company and we did. Both of us. End of story."

"Maybe just the beginning of story, Noble Student. What did you learn from those relationships?"

"That I'm probably not good marriage material."

"Oh, I hope you learned more than that."

"Well, I learned that I don't often choose wisely…"

"And…?"

"And what?"

"And when you don't, you stay in the relationship because there is a significant amount of fear when you think of change, of altering the status quo, as it were, no matter how painful it might be. I mean you stay with Elaine for two years after her bizarre behavior started. Two years, Edward."

"That's not exactly true. It would be more accurate to say that I have some fear, some…trepidation, mild trepidation, about change."

"Here's what I bet happened. When Elaine left, you called Margaret, the midget marrying jewel junkie…Oh, I like that phrase. The midget marrying jewel junkie. Be sure and include that."

"Everything goes in, Tyler. You know that. Even the four letter words."

"Anyway, you probably called Margaret just to see what she was up to. You may even have considered asking her out if she was available at the moment. I mean midgets come and go."

"How did you know that?"

"Because that's what I did after *my* second divorce. My first wife's name was Betty and I remember thinking, *Hey, maybe we can get back together.* In fact, she didn't want anything to do with me."

"Hard to believe, Maestro."

"Believe, Edward. You know I really think we should get practice wives and practice children for at least the first five years of marriage. Maybe robots so that when we screw them up we can take them back to the factory to get re-programmed. That way maybe we wouldn't harm so many people."

"You didn't do well with Betty?"

"No," he said. "But it didn't stop me from blaming her for a lot of the stuff that went on."

"I'm not blaming anyone. I'm just explaining why…"

"The point is that when my marriage to Martha hit the skids, I wanted to go back instead of forward. Safer, I thought."

"You think I do that?"

"I do," he said. "But what I think doesn't make a whole lot of difference. What do you think?"

"I'm…considering the possibility that I might have some small amount of resistance to change. Very small."

"While you're at it you might want to consider your job situation."

"I'm Mr. Stability when it comes to my job, Tyler. You know that. I've had the same job for twelve years."

"Why?"

"Why?…Well…Because I'm a good employee, that's one reason. A worker among workers. A…"

"But you hate your job."

"Hate is probably too strong a word. Dislike sometimes maybe, but…"

"No, you actually hate your job. I've heard you say it dozens of times. It's either the management at Safeway or the customers or the entire stupid industry that is purposely aligned against you to make your life miserable. Now, the question is simple—why would you continue to work at a job you hate?"

"…I don't think that's such a simple question."

"The answer may be complex," said Tyler, "but the question is very simple. Why would you continue to work at a job you hate?"

"Because I like to eat on a regular basis."

"Poor excuse to work at a job you hate."

"It is?"

"Definitely."

"I could request disability and have the State support me, like some other individuals of my acquaintance."

"And your disability would be...?"

"I have a...broken Coping Mechanism."

"Request denied," he said.

"Maybe you'd like to support me, Tyler. You could take me as a deduction. Sole support. I could cook, clean the house, even mow the lawn on occasion."

"I'm too old and mean to live with," he said.

"I have no trouble believing that."

"And I also have several ex-wives who will testify to the arbitrary nature of my temperament and how difficult I was to live with. But let me restate the question, lest we get too far off track. Why would you continue to work at a job you hate?"

"You want me to say it's because I'm afraid of change, don't you? Isn't that what you're driving at?"

"I'm not driving at anything. I'm just asking a question. Why do you always think I'm trying to get you to say something?"

"Because you're highly manipulative, Tyler."

"Not true," he said.

"Trust me. I know manipulation when I see it."

"You think I'm being manipulative by asking why you've spent twelve years working at a job you hate?"

"See?" I said. "You're still doing it."

"You ever hear the thing about the only difference between a rut and the grave is a matter of depth?"

"I don't think that's funny."

"It's not supposed to be funny, Edward."

"I'm very aware of what I'm doing, Tyler. Very cognizant of my place on the path."

"So what would you really like to do? I mean instead of ringing up packages of Ball Park Franks and six packs of Coors and dealing with the Great Unwashed all day long."

"...I'd like to be published and famous. Rich wouldn't hurt either."

"So here you are writing," said Tyler. "And as soon as *The Seven Deadly Needs* gets into print, you'll be a published author. *Voila!*"

"This is not writing, Tyler. This is transcribing. Or retyping. I mean I want to do some creative writing."

"Then do it."

"...Just do it?"

"Yes. Make a schedule. Set some priorities. Write every day. Befriend the demons of doubt. Just do it."

"I don't think I know how."

"No excuse," he said. "Here's some sage advice from Tennessee Williams:

> There is a time for departure even when there's
> no certain place to go.

"But..."

"If you do what you've always done, you'll get what you've always gotten. Ever hear that? It's an extension of that famous equation—No change equals no change. Perfect symmetry."

"But where would I start? And how?"

"You start with the willingness. Change something. Anything. Start brushing your teeth left-handed. Take a different route to work. Sit down at the typewriter, or with your big yellow legal pad, or in front of a computer and just start writing a story. Any story."

"Shouldn't I maybe take a writing class and learn how?"

"You already know how to do it, Edward. You know how to write. What you're doing now is getting ready to get ready to get ready. Delaying tactics thinly disguised as preparation. You're trapped in a room full of mirrors and you've become convinced that just one more image will complete the picture. No way. Just do it."

"Just start?"

"What have you got to lose?"

"But…"

"I'll admit it's a little scary," said Tyler. "But the alternative to facing the fear of change, the alternative to action, is to hunker down in your own little phone booth and watch the world go by as you think about the possibility of making a phone call. Safe but not much fun. *There's a time for departure even when there's no certain place to go.*"

"…I don't know."

"Think of it as another Serenity Prayer issue."

"Tyler, you think everything's a Serenity Prayer issue."

"Because it is…We ask for the serenity to accept the things we can't change, right?"

"Right," I said.

"The courage to change the things we can, and the wisdom to know the difference."

"So?"

"So, once we decide what things we can change," he said, "we ask for the courage to actually change them."

"Ask who?"

"Start with the Great Pumpkin if that works for you."

"And if it doesn't?"

"The Force, Allah, God, Great Spirit, whatever you're comfortable with. It doesn't make any difference."

"It doesn't?"

"No," he said. "You think God cares?"

"What I think is that you have some very strange ideas about what religion is supposed to be like."

"Stop dancing around the God thing. You have this preconceived notion of what God should be, and you discard everything that doesn't fit the form. Truth is, nobody really knows. I mean for sure. You're simply avoiding the issue."

"Which is what?"

"Change, Noble Student. Fear of change, of new situations. Fear of failure is also a big factor. I may not be great at what I'm doing but at least I'm not a complete failure. And if I change, if I embark on a new venture…what then?"

"I'm not avoiding change, Tyler. I'm just being careful. Cautious."

"No, you're stubbornly refusing to look at the possibility that you have a terrible fear of change."

"But what if I try to change, start writing or doing something I really want to do and find out that I can't? That I'm no good at it. What then?"

"Is it better not knowing?" said Tyler. "Would you rather go through life thinking, *I could have done that if I had really tried?* Or, *I always wanted to do that, but…now it's too late.*"

"I don't know…"

"You know what people regret when they're dying?"

"No."

"They regret the things they *haven't* done," said Tyler. "Not the things they've done."

"You still volunteer at the Hospice on Fridays?"

"Yeah."

"That's what people tell you?"

"It is."

"Man…"

"I remember a guy there not long ago whose one big regret in life was that he'd never taken that boat trip down the Amazon River. That's all he talked about. Had the chance to do it when he was young, but found lots of reasons why he couldn't. Too much money, too little time, too something."

"And now it's too late."

"Yeah," said Tyler. "Too late…And what if you do try to write and it turns out you're not the next Great American Novelist? Isn't it worth knowing? I mean instead of lamenting what might have been? Maybe you're a weaver. Or a plumber. A carpenter. Maybe the most prolific, unpublished writer in the history of American letters. Maybe you're supposed to sit with dying people and hold their hands while they make the transition. You'll be making a contribution, helping to change the world. It doesn't make any difference what it is. Just do it."

"My head hurts, Tyler. Did I catch it from you?"

"I leave you with a timely quote from Arthur Benson. I've been saving it just for you."

"Oh, boy."

"…*Very often a change of self is needed more than a change of scene.*"

"Goodnight, Tyler."

"Goodnight, Edward. I trust that courage will attend your efforts."

"I know one about change."

"Tell," he said.

"*All is changing save the law of change*…Heraclitus."

"Well done, my friend. Goodnight."

CHAPTER 5

FEAR OF FAILURE, REJECTION & ABANDONMENT

Success is going from failure to failure
without loss of enthusiasm. . . .

Sir Winston Churchill

"You know, I thought about what we talked about last week," I said.

"Good. And just what was it you thought about it?"

"I thought about how ironic it was that we talked about making changes and that's what I do all day—I make change. At Safeway."

"And...?"

"Get it? Making change...Making changes."

"Oh..."

"You remember, we talked about making changes. Last week? And that's what I do all..."

"I got it, Edward. No need to belabor the point. It's just that there wasn't much to get, that's all."

"Tyler, sometimes I think you're the worst person in the entire world. The absolute worst."

"And just why do you think that?"

"You'll notice that I said it twice, the worst person part. For emphasis. A well-known literary device I thought you might appreciate…"

"You think your reaction has something to do with how you feel about criticism?" said Tyler.

"Nothing wrong with my reaction. And I'm not afraid of being criticized. I've got skin like a rhinoceros."

"Bullets and bad words just bounce right off, eh?"

"I put up with it all day at Safeway. I get blamed because things cost too much, because the bananas are green and never ripen no matter how long they let them sit in that brown paper bag by the window—I mean people actually do that, get on my case about green bananas and how they don't get ripe, like it's my fault. And some people just seem to be having a bad day and think it's okay to rip the checker at Safeway instead of waiting to get home and take it out on the dog or the kids or the spousal unit."

"But you're offended because you think I criticized you," said Tyler.

"Just because I said you might be the worst person in the entire world? That why you think that?"

"I thought that might have something to do with it."

"For the record, Tyler, I don't actually think you're the worst person in the entire world. I want to get that on the tape. It's a small exaggeration. Not the entire world. Most of it maybe, but not all of it. There may be others who are worse. Somewhere."

"So what's the fear that we're hiding in this conversation?"

"There has to be a fear?"

"Not necessarily," he said. "But in this case, I think yes. I was going to suggest that we talk about the fear of failure this week, and maybe the fear of criticism is a natural lead in…"

"Did I tell you I went out with someone new last week? Had a date with someone I'd never been out with."

"…Just how did we get from the fear of criticism to your most recent dating experience?"

"Easy," I said. "Weren't we talking about the fear of change last week?"

"We were."

"Well, here I am forging ahead, not looking back, after my last disastrous relationship with the hideous Teresa Wendover. I thought you'd approve."

"I do," said Tyler. "I do. What's the name of your new …adventure."

"Oh…You wouldn't know her."

"I might," said Tyler.

"Her name's Holly."

"I see. Just one name? Like Madonna? Or Britney?"

"…Holly Brobeck."

"Huh…"

"So…? You know her?"

"No, I don't think so."

"You're lying, Tyler. It's written all over your face. You forget how well I know you. If you don't tell me, I'll be forced to do something evil and reprehensible to you."

"For a minute there I thought it might have been another lady I knew named Dolly."

"*Holly*," I said. "With an H…As in hobbyhorse. Or hormone. Your hearing aid batteries gone again? You should try those Energizer things. They just keep going and going and going and going and going…"

Tyler ignored the dig, which was unlike him. When he begins to look at some imaginary spot about a foot over my head, I know something's coming.

"You like her?"

"Holly? Yeah, I like her...Is this energy medicine lady affiliated in any way with the Energizer Bunny?"

"What is it you like about her?"

"She's pretty. She's..."

"She's young, right?"

"She might be," I said. "Actually I didn't notice much. I mean she's probably younger than that Dolly Madison you're referring to, who would be somewhere around a hundred and fifty by now."

"Really young," said Tyler.

"I didn't ask for ID, but she's at least voting age. I'm guessing twentyish. Maybe older."

"You met her on the internet?"

"...Maybe we should get back to the fear-of-the-week. What did you say it was?"

"I think we mentioned the fear of criticism, fear of failure, abandonment maybe. You think they're related? The fears? I have a hunch that..."

"What difference does it make if I met her on the internet? There are perfectly legitimate people who use the internet all the time. Who post ads on the internet every day. Get married and have babies. Good God-fearing people from Iowa and Kansas. Middle America. Corn fed, wholesome. The salt of the earth. Tipper Gore probably uses the internet, for chrissakes."

"I don't think you have to defend your use of the internet, Edward," he said. "I wasn't attacking you, or criticizing you, or suggesting that you might be a failure."

"Well I'm certainly not a failure, Tyler. As you well know. Those three marriages, though not particularly long in duration, were packed with very intense and sometimes even loving moments. I made every attempt to make things work out. And if we're talking about blame, there was certainly enough to go around for everyone involved. As for my career, I'm at the top of my game. I get great reviews every year, and, as I'm sure you remember, I was voted one of the Top Ten Safeway Employees at the regional meeting in Cheyenne just last year."

"Did I hit a sensitive spot, Edward?"

"No. Of course not. I'm just explaining how far off the mark you are, that's all."

"Just when I thought I was getting a handle on things," said Tyler, shaking his head. "What I wanted to say, just in case you're thinking about owning up to your feelings about it anytime soon, is that I hate criticism, too. Absolutely hate it. I still think criticism is ridicule. All criticism. As far as I'm concerned, there's no such thing as constructive criticism."

"...Really?"

"When people find it necessary to criticize something I'm doing, I immediately begin devising new methods of torture. Immediately. No hesitation at all on my part."

"I'm amazed. I thought you were beyond all that."

"I used to think so, too. And by the way, be careful of people who have gone beyond and transcended the human condition—the emotionally bulletproof. Those who have, so to speak, *arrived*. They can be very dangerous. You remember who said, *Believe those who seek the truth; doubt those who find it?*"

"...Nixon?"

"No," he said. "I'll help. It wasn't Nixon and it wasn't Jesus. Or Shakespeare."

"George W?

"No."

"Then I'm out of guesses."

"Andre Gide."

"Of course…Andre."

"And I'm sure you remember the book I lent you last year, *If You Meet the Buddha on the Road, Kill Him?*"

"I do."

"That's your answer. Just be careful."

"I'm *en garde*, as Andre might say."

"So, back to the fears. I've come to realize that my inability to accept any kind of criticism is just one of the many character defects I'll carry to the grave with me. Think about the *Progress, not perfection* we talked about. I think I've mentioned some of them—the character defects. Check the tape on *The Seven Deadly Needs.*"

"My hero has feet of clay?"

"And hands of clay," said Tyler. "Sometimes I think a heart of clay…very earthbound. Please understand, Noble Student, that all this, this thing we call Life, is a process, not an event. If you want all your fears, all your character defects, to go away the minute you acknowledge them and ask the Great Pumpkin to remove them, you're in for a big disappointment."

"You…earthbound? That's not what I hear. There are some pretty spooky tales out there about you floating around in the ether, sharing space with all those guru types."

"Actually, me being earthbound is the good news. Although there was a time…there was a time when I thought I was scaling the spiritual heights, sharing the rarified air with assorted gurus and ascended Masters…before tumbling unceremoniously back to earth."

"How so?"

"You see, Edward, this thing about being a spiritual giant is highly overrated. Even the attempt is dangerous. For one thing, it separates me from my brothers and sisters. From the community that I love. Turns out there's no one to share the terrors of living with. The fears. The glaring defects that don't seem to go away no matter what I do. There's just you and your...followers, for lack of a better word. And everybody wants you to be bulletproof because they think that if they can become bulletproof they'll be safe. Just like you. So they want to believe that you're invulnerable. That you've somehow arrived, become one of the Elect and now live on a mountaintop impervious to the painful slings and arrows of everyday living. Romance and finance problems cannot possibly penetrate the shield of sanctity you've developed. And you want to believe it, too. You want to live up to their expectations. You want to believe it's all true. But when the closet door opens at three in the morning and all those ...things rush out, you know it's not true."

"Things?" I said.

"Demons. You know."

"You could do your Milarepa trick and invite them to stay for tea."

"It was long ago, Edward. Long before I knew much of anything. I was poorly armed with a little knowledge and a lot of spiritual arrogance."

"So what did you do?"

"I turned in my guru badge," said Tyler. "Started telling people what it was really like. What *I* was really like. For most people it was not a popular decision. They had to go find another guru."

"I didn't know any of that."

"It was in my younger years, when I wanted to be what people thought I was. All the while carefully orchestrating what it was I wanted them to believe about me, scheming to create the illusion that I had looked into the eye of the tiger and survived, that I had had deep and meaningful spiritual experiences leading sometimes to episodes of levitation but please don't tell anyone. Not yet, anyway…And that, if I wasn't actually one of the ascended Masters, I was close enough to be considered among the Elect."

"Man. Live and learn, eh?"

"Hopefully."

"So tell me about the fear of criticism," I said.

"For me it was never being able to do things right," he said. "To do anything right. You remember the story I told you about Serenity Sam?"

"Only vaguely," I said.

"Let me refresh your memory."

"Nothing wrong with my memory."

"Sorry."

"Nothing wrong with my memory."

"Okay, okay…Serenity Sam and his buddy Big Red had been out drinking for several days, and one night, looking for a place to sleep, they crawled into the back seat of an old car in that junk yard down on Franklin. Well, the story goes, at least according to Sam, that Big Red woke up the next morning, looked out the car window at the junk yard with all those rusty old cars and upside-down bathtubs and said, *My God, Sam, they've thrown us away.*"

"Jeez…"

"You ever feel like that?" said Tyler. "Like a throw-away?"

"Man…"

"You know, crying is allowed."

"I'm not crying, Tyler."

"Just in case you do," he said. "Or you feel like it."

"I never cry."

"I know that. I'm just reinforcing the notion that all types of feelings are allowed. Encouraged even. You remember the thing about Experience Follows Expectations that we talked about?"

"Yeah."

"Here's another one—Feelings Follow Beliefs. Feelings express emotional reactions to beliefs."

"Slow down, Maestro. I'm still digesting the story. I mean I know them, both those guys. I can imagine Red looking out that window and saying that…So what's the lesson?"

"Or the fear," he said.

"Okay, the fear. What are we trying to get at?"

"We're trying to get at the reasons behind why the fear of criticism is so difficult for some of us. So emotionally crippling. Does it automatically lead to feelings of being a failure, being expendable, a throwaway? How about the fear of abandonment?"

"Hence the junkyard story," I said.

"The perfect metaphor. What was it the young kids in recovery used to say? *God don't make no junk?*"

"Right."

"So what pops up in your memory bank when you think about criticism? What fear is attached to it that makes it so hard to accept any kind of criticism?"

"Failure, mostly. That somehow I didn't get it right. Again…But, you know, when I think about it, about my reactions to stuff like that, they all seem out of proportion."

"How so?" said Tyler.

"I mean there must be tons of kids who went through the same things I went through and didn't turn out to be as nuts as I am."

"But you, having a Broken Brain which reacts to most events by going to the Worst Case Scenario, respond in ways that are not always what people would consider normal. Or appropriate. Tell them about the thumb sucking, Edward."

"Did I tell you about that?"

"You did."

68

"Perhaps a poor decision," I said.

"You remember that part of the deal we made?"

"Yeah. I have to tell you everything."

"That's the deal," he said. "Everything, no matter how sordid or embarrassing or childish it may seem."

"That's what Father Hopkins used to say in the confessional…*That everything, son? And just where did you touch her? How many times? Did you spill the seed?* Always had to know about spilling the seed. *Is she a Catholic girl, son*…Apparently, it was less sinful if she was Protestant, because she had already been consigned to the depths of hell because she *was* a Protestant. And we all knew what Martin Luther did that screwed everything up. Wasn't for him *everybody* would be Catholic. Except maybe the Jews. They never told us about the Buddhists or the Moslems or the others. Maybe they figured we wouldn't notice."

"That's the deal—everything."

"And we have that deal because?…Sometimes I have trouble remembering why I have to tell you everything."

"Because I'm your sponsor, your mentor, if you will. And mentors get paid the big bucks to listen as you begin to process your life, your recovery, and in that process, learn to live a more productive life without killing yourself or injuring loved ones or innocent bystanders who might get sprayed with all that emotional shrapnel when you open the shoebox with the memories in it. If you withhold information from your mentor, or worse yet, lie to your mentor, the Great Pumpkin will come down and eat your nose."

"I remember now. Simple but not easy."

"That's it," he said. "Back to the thumb. Did it make you feel better?"

"It was…comforting is probably the right word. But then they put that awful tasting stuff on it so I wouldn't have it in my mouth all the time."

"You take a lot of heat for that?" said Tyler.

"You can imagine what kids say when you've got your thumb stuck in your mouth all the time. The girls just giggled, but the guys came up with very inventive interpretations, new ones nearly every day."

"I can imagine," said Tyler.

"I finally stopped, but then chewed my fingernails down to the quick for the next twenty years."

"Guess you showed them."

"But you know I did play football in high school."

"Yeah?"

"Mostly to prove I wasn't a sissy. I mean I figured there weren't a lot of sissies playing football. And of course my father thought I should play. Macho Man himself. But I was good. Junior year I was second team all-league."

"And you hated every minute of it."

"I did. I was terrified all the time. But my father loved it and my mother worried, so I got a lot of attention."

"And not much criticism."

"Not much. Until I quit just before my senior year. Man…Talk about heat. I got it from the coach, the other kids, my father, everybody."

"And you quit because…?"

"Because one night, after I had a few drinks and smoked a little non-habit forming marijuana for the first time, I had a vision of what life could be like. It was amazing; like I had suddenly discovered some magic elixir. I had never imagined that life could be so beautiful. A few drinks, a little Happy Weed and I simply didn't care anymore. Trouble was, I didn't seem to know when to stop, even after the highs became lows. Then later I discovered that I *couldn't* stop. I operated under the assumption that if a little bit was good, more was better."

"The old More-Is-Better School of Addiction."

"It seemed perfectly logical."

"It does, doesn't it. And the criticism?"

"Background noise, though I was still aware of it."

"But you still felt like a failure," said Tyler.

"Yeah. Failures do things like quit the football team, get lousy grades, bite their nails, get drunk, disappoint all kinds of people. That's what failures do. That's what I did."

"Let me suggest that living up to other peoples' expectations is a lifetime job that can only end in futility. It's living life from the outside in. And you know what happens when people criticize things and judge them to be failures?"

"What?"

"They...discard them. Abandon them, reject them, they throw-them-away. Bye, bye, thing. Or person. Especially old person. Foreign person. Person of a different color. Useless. Into the trash. The progression goes like this—find fault, criticize, reject, throw away, abandon."

"The sequence is familiar."

"You see, Edward, for whatever the reason, or reasons, I grew up with a papier mâché interior life just like you did. Maybe it's part of the whole Broken Brain thing. A house of cards. A flimsy structure made out of matchsticks. The first emotional upset, the first blow, the first *criticism* destroyed whatever fragile balance I had managed to acquire. It became that familiar hole in my stomach with the cold wind blowing through."

"So when criticism rears its ugly head...all the buttons get pushed."

"They do," said Tyler. "And criticism is just another word for failure to some of us. And of course failure is just a short step from rejection and abandonment...and the closet."

"...A-mazing."

"Truly. And I am suggesting in the gentlest possible way that you may have chosen young Miss Holly to some degree

71

because of her age and the fact that at that tender age she would certainly be less likely to criticize or find fault with a person of your stature...and age."

"Of course that's not a criticism."

"God forbid."

"So the solution is...?"

"You're halfway there if you've acknowledged the fear. There's something in a book by Marianne Williamson that you should read. It starts with, *Our deepest fear is not that we are inadequate* and ends with *As we are liberated from our fears, our presence automatically liberates others.* It's only a few lines. Read it every day till we get together next week."

"Where can I find it?"

"Ask the Great Pumpkin."

"Jeez, Tyler..."

"If that fails, check the internet. Maybe you can find something else besides a teenage date. But...enough for this week, my friend. I've got to do the laundry."

"Don't forget the hearing aid batteries."

"The what?"

"Don't forget the..."

"Just kidding, Edward. See you next week."

"I'm counting on it. You know what we're going to talk about?"

"...How about loss of control. Being unable to take care of yourself. How does that sound."

"Frightening."

"Good. See you next week."

"Goodnight, Maestro."

"...Goodnight."

CHAPTER 6

FEAR OF LOSING CONTROL, BEING A BURDEN

"Fear is the prison of the heart."
Anonymous.

"What do you think the survey says is one of the top three fears?"

"What survey?"

"The Family Feud Survey," said Tyler. "You don't watch Family Feud?"

"It's still on?"

"Reruns, I think. Bad teevee shows never die, Edward."

"You know, I have a friend who swears she saw you coming out of that movie theater over on Broadway the other night. The Gothic, I think. Isn't that the one that shows those low budget porno films?"

"Does your mind just leap from place to place without reference to the conversation?"

"I just thought of it so I had to say it. If I let it slide, I know I'll forget it. That's called insight—basically knowing what my limitations are."

"I don't know what it's called," said Tyler, "but I don't think insight is the right word. Besides, it's redundant."

"What's redundant?"

"Low budget and porno," said Tyler. "Porno films are, by definition, low budget."

"So it *was* you...God, Tyler..."

"First of all, Noble Student, the Gothic doesn't show porno films. Or rarely does. It shows classic films like *The Bicycle Thief, How Green Was My Valley, All The King's Men*...Occasionally we get a Frankenstein or Werewolf movie. I remember one vampire movie—*Nosferatu.*"

"Talkies?"

"Mostly," said Tyler. "Although *City Lights* is one of my all-time favorites and it's a silent movie."

"Not exactly my kind of movies. I'm more the Bruce Willis, Arnold Schwarzenegger type. Adventure with a little mindless violence thrown in."

"You like the beat-'em-up, blow-'em-ups?"

"Mostly...Anyway, my friend says it was something like two in the morning when she saw you."

"The classic films series are usually midnight shows," he said.

"I thought you went to bed early."

"Doesn't get much earlier than two A.M."

"No, I mean..."

"Truth is, I have to take a nap in the afternoon or I can't stay awake."

"So my aging hero has to take a nap before he shuffles off to some silent movie. Or monster flick. That it? And you go by yourself? I have this awful picture of you trudging alone down on lower Broadway in a pathetic gray overcoat to get your fill of on-screen gore at the Gothic. I can imagine what the clientele is like."

"Not bad, Edward, though the horror films seem to attract a dress up crowd. When they show a vampire movie, everybody shows up as a vampire. Everybody."

"You, too?"

"Well...I do have a cape. That's usually enough so I don't appear conspicuous."

"You go alone?"

"Not always," said Tyler. "Sometimes I..."

"You take Mercedes, right? That's it. I knew it. Mercedes really *is* a witch and you both go and take in these late night...rituals. What else do you guys do?"

"I do go with Mercedes on occasion, and no, she's not a witch."

"Man...I don't know what to make of..."

"It's just information, Edward. Perhaps there's really nothing to make of it. I find life endlessly fascinating, that's all. The midnight version as well as the noontime version."

"You don't talk much about it, about what your midnight version was like. Or *is* like. And how come *you* don't have to tell *me* everything?"

"It wasn't pleasant. Mercedes has helped me process some of it; some of the midnight version. But I can't think of anything we can't discuss—you and I. Or is it you and me?"

"Either way," I said. "I never remember which is right."

"Anyway, we can get into that next week if you'd like to. Next week is the fear of dying, the fear of being in pain. We saved some of the best for last."

"And this week is what?"

"Fear of becoming a burden, losing control of your life. Being in a position where other people have to take care of you."

"That's my mother," I said. "She hates having people do things for her."

"But she can't do them for herself anymore, right?"

"Right."

"And she still hates having other people do them for her. She resents them?"

"Big time. She has a huge resentment against poor Mrs. Gallagher, who comes every Tuesday and Thursday to clean up and cook lunch. She may actually like Mrs. Gallagher, but you'd never know it by the way she talks about her. Or treats her."

"It's the old payback thing," said Tyler, "another one of the Great American Myths about independence and self-reliance. Our cultural heritage from the Old West. If you're doing things for me, helping me because I can't help myself anymore, then I'm going to owe you big time and I simply can't bear the thought. It's The Scorekeeper meets the Control Freak, in living color."

"That's my mom."

"Branches of this fear have to do with the fact that if I can't *do* much then I'm not *worth* much because, at least in this country, most people would have me believe that *I Am What I Do*, and if I'm not doing much, I'm not worth much. I'm simply a burden, a drag on the social system, more to be scorned than to be helped. The Scorekeeper in me tells me I'm losing, and the Control Freak laments the fact that I can't do a thing about it. An impossible situation."

"So what's the message?"

"The message is that my value, my worth as a human being, is equal to my ability to contribute."

"Contribute meaning...?"

"Some arbitrary, socially defined, measure of my use-fulness. It may be the ability to work and make money, the more money the better, to have a special skill, the ability to raise children—though that's a little out of style—to function without outside help, anything having to do with being self-sufficient rather than being on the receiving end of some local or federal handout program."

"And all this leads to what?"

"Leads to the following question: If I am what I do and I'm not doing anything, what am I?"

"You're a zero...a nobody."

"Precisely, my dear Watson. A no-body. A non-entity. I step on the scale, the social scale, but it doesn't register anything because basically, I don't exist. And even though I'm invisible, it costs money to keep me invisible. I'm like the homeless, the street people. We simply don't see them anymore."

"My mom has this thing about people who try to help her," I said. "She always manages to find fault with whoever I send. She informed me that one of the ladies I had the agency send up was black, like that was a big surprise—wow, a black lady. Never seen one of those before. Another one was fat; she didn't like her either. Maybe the black lady was even fat; she didn't say. My mother's got a shape like a dumpling, so I don't know what she has against fat ladies. But it's always something."

"Probably doesn't have anything to do with black ladies or fat ladies. It would have been the same no matter who the agency sent."

"You think?"

"Sure," said Tyler. "And it may have more to do with trust than anything else. In all likelihood she doesn't trust any of those people you send to help her. Why should she? As a woman who was born in the twenties, she has had very little reason to trust anyone. She's afraid of losing control, being helpless and having strangers take care of her. How would you feel if some stranger was trooping through your apartment every other day, fussing with your stuff, telling you what to do?"

"If it was some fox from Baywatch I wouldn't mind."

"How about some three hundred pounder in a flowery muumuu from the Saturday Night Tractor Pull?"

"I'd probably be less...receptive."

"I bet," said Tyler.

"Point made," I said. "You know, she made me promise never to send her to a nursing home."

"You promise?"

"I did. And she has these signs all over the house that say Do Not Resuscitate. Has one on the door to the bedroom. Even has one on the lampshade by her bed."

"Please don't help, eh? I'm...just...fine."

"But the strange part is that when she thought she was having a heart attack, she called 911 then hid all the signs before they got there."

"She wants to die on her own terms, that's all. And, don't underestimate the importance of the fact that *she* made the call. She was in control. Plus the fact that people make a big fuss over her when she calls 911. Sirens, ambulance, people rushing through the building with life-saving equipment. You make a fuss over your mother?"

"Not often," I said. "I mean I go see her once in awhile. I call. You know."

"But you don't make a big fuss. You love your mother?"

"Tyler, what does that have to do with this fear thing we're talking about?"

"So you love your mother?"

"Jeez...Yes, I love my mother."

"But you don't like her very much."

"True. I don't like her very much. In fact, she's not very likeable. She's the most passive-aggressive person I've ever known. When I try to get close to her she hits me with that

Mommy-Knows-Best Hatchet she keeps hidden in the folds of her pioneer dress. She does the same thing to my two sisters, neither of whom will go see her. Or even talk to her."

"Being able to receive is one of the toughest assignments that life has for us," said Tyler. "It means I'm a burden, someone who can't take care of himself. Or herself. I have absolutely no control over what's going on. You know how to receive?"

"Sure. You want to give me some money? Try me out? See how well I receive a couple of c-notes?"

"You remember asking for anything recently?'

"I ask for things all the time."

"Like for instance?" said Tyler.

"Well...I ask for the check at a restaurant when I eat out. At least sometimes. Pass the salt. The pepper. Butter. Things like that."

"Bravo. And not *too* risky, I'd think."

"I'm sure there are other things, Tyler. I just can't come up with a bunch off the top of my head."

"It's a grace to be able to receive."

"A grace meaning what?" I said. "That seems like a very theological word for you to be using."

"Grace is an unmerited gift."

"Explanation follows?"

"Some form of help given by the Great Spirit or the Great Pumpkin to enable you to do something."

"Like receive?" I said.

"In this case."

"And how do I go about getting this unmerited gift?"

"I thought we'd never get to that part," said Tyler. "It's very simple. You ask."

"Ask. Would that be prayer we're referring to?"

"If you want to label a request like that prayer, that's up to you. I just use ask. I consider the Great Pumpkin one of the Primary Sources of Power, who, unfortunately, might not be a mind reader. So, to be on the safe side, I need to ask."

"Doesn't The Great Pumpkin know everything."

"That's what I heard," said Tyler.

"Then why would I have to ask?"

"Just part of the deal, Edward. One of the rules. The message seems to be, *Ask and you shall receive.* So you have to ask. Even if the Great Pumpkin already knows, you have to ask. I don't make up the rules."

"Man..."

"It's like epoxy," said Tyler. "We have two things—the desire on one hand and the power on the other. If you don't get the two together, nothing happens. Inertsville. You can have lots of desire but nothing's going to happen until you get the mojo, the juice, to go with it and actually get something done. And you get the mojo by asking."

"....Inertsville?"

"I just made that up," said Tyler. "Like it?"

"Let's get back to the fears, Maestro. I'm lost."

"Fear not, as the saying goes. We're not as far off course as you might imagine. A minor digression about the fear of losing control. All relevant, Noble Student. All connected to feelings of powerlessness, being at the mercy of others, losing control. Takes great trust and faith. I ever tell you I went to Lourdes a few years ago?"

"The shrine? In France?"

"Right."

"You're just chock full of surprises tonight," I said. "First it's the classic/horror movies that you sneak off to see at midnight with Mercedes the Witch. Now it's holy shrines you're visiting. So why Lourdes?"

"Well, I had gone to see my son Steve in Spain and I wasn't all that far away. So I took a side trip."

"Didn't you get enough of that stuff in Catholic school?"

"Doesn't have anything to do with religion. Lourdes is about believing, about trust, knowing it's okay to be a burden, about letting other people take care of you. Allowing other people to be of service."

"You see any miracles?"

"I didn't see anybody toss their crutches away and dance down the street, but I saw miracles."

"So I'm ready for a miracle story, Maestro."

"These are not the take-up-your-bed-and-walk type of stories, Edward. These are...different. If you listen with your heart you'll be able to hear better."

"Roger," I said. "Turning on the heart. Proceed with story."

"First of all, being there helps."

"You mean there's more...mojo if you're actually there."

"Right. The place radiates some kind of...energy. Or power. I don't know what to call it, but you can feel it. What you see mostly are people in wheelchairs being pushed around by volunteers who are all smiling as if they're in on some secret. They're so...devotional about it. And happy. Happy about pushing the wheelchairs. Imagine. Like it's the most important thing in the world. And even some of the sick people have that same look. It's all very orderly, very processional, solemn yet somehow upbeat. The sick are wheeled into these...places where they wait patiently to get lowered into the water. Then wheeled back to...I guess wherever they came from."

"The trash heap."

"I don't think so. Then there's the grotto nearby where Mary was supposed to have appeared."

"You believe that? That she appeared?"

81

"I don't know," said Tyler. "I believe in the possibility of everything. But I believe that those kids believed; Bernadette and those other two kids who were there. I believe that they believed. I don't know about the rest of it; about whether anyone else appeared."

"Glory be, Tyler."

"But there's something there—at Lourdes. Some... power, mystery, some force for lack of a better word. I actually got some of the water in a little vial to take with me."

"Hoping for a miracle cure, or just something to put in your prune juice in the morning?"

He usually just ignores me when I get really flaky.

"...I didn't know what to make of it," he said. "Still don't. I expected something different. I was led to believe it was pure chaos—noisy, people pushing and shoving and shouting, all trying to get into the water first. But it wasn't like that at all. It just struck me that these people had such great patience and trust and faith."

"In the Great Pumpkin?"

"Whatever you want to call It. They somehow knew that being powerless or being what we call a burden was perfectly all right. It was in itself a gift that they gave to others, like the volunteers, so that they could all participate in this particular miracle. Acceptance in its purest form...I even said a prayer that my oldest son would get sober."

"Tommy?"

"Yeah. Thomas Charles," said Tyler. "My bright, young, blue-eyed left-hander who could never seem to get his arms around life."

"Didn't you tell me he died a couple of years ago?"

"Rollover car accident. Almost a year to the day when I was at Lourdes."

"...And you still talk to God?"

"The Great Pumpkin."

"Even the Great Pumpkin."

"Prayers get answered in strange ways," said Tyler.

"You think Tommy's death was the answer to the prayer? Tyler, please…"

"I think it was *one* answer. Maybe it happened the only way it could have happened."

"Jeez…You know, crying's allowed."

"I knew that. I may have even said that on occasion."

"…You have."

"Anyway, I think Tommy just decided earth life wasn't for him anymore. So he's driving along highway 10 on his way to Phoenix in the middle of the afternoon, falls asleep, loses control, car rolls over four times and he dies instantly. Broken neck. No seat belt. Nobody else in the car. Thomas Charles Tyler. I named him after a couple of drunks—the Welsh poet, Dylan Thomas and my father, Charles. Kid probably never had a chance."

"Man…Did it make you crazy?"

"…For awhile."

"And then…?"

"Finally had to let it go. You can only hold on to something like that for so long. You know, Serenity Prayer stuff. Acceptance. Surrender. Let go. You know the drill."

"I do."

"But he shows up in my morning meditation sometimes —Tommy does. In dreams, too. He and my father, who died long before Tommy was born. Died when I was in my early twenties. Cirrhosis. My father and my son, both on the Other Side."

"…You want to go out and get some pizza, Maestro?"

"No. I ate at the Olive Garden on the way over," said Tyler. "And I'm a little weary. Maybe it's old age."

"What'd you have to eat."

"Lasagna.

"That explains it. Lasagna's very heavy. That Italian food's what made all those Popes so tough to get along with. Very heavy duty. Try some salad next time."

"You know, the older I get, the less I know," said Tyler. "When I was young, I was sure I had all the answers. Now..."

"Don't tell me about how little you know, Tyler. Because if you don't know much, where does that leave me? I'm relying on you to have answers."

"Tricky proposition."

"What is?"

"Answers. Truth..."

"I think you'd better go home and hit the sack. Get some rest. I hope you're not going out with Mercedes tonight."

"No," said Tyler. "We talked about going to see *The Lost Weekend,* but neither of us is in the mood."

"Maybe you can go out and pull your vampire maneuver. Find some young thing with a nice plump neck to sink your teeth into. Perhaps a little blond with Type A blood. Something to boost your energy level. Mercedes could help—hold her down while you drained her."

"Nothing quite so dramatic, Edward. Just the laundry tonight. You ever read that book by Jack Kornfield? *After the Ecstasy, the Laundry?*"

"No."

"I'll lend you my copy. Very instructive. Reminds me of an old saying:

> *Before enlightenment, chop wood and carry water.*
> *After enlightenment, chop wood and carry water.*

"Get some sleep, Maestro. It's not true that the older you get, the less sleep you need. Go home and rest. I'll see you next week."

"For the final episode…"

"No, no, not final. Just the last of the seven. Drive carefully and stay out of the fast lane. And don't leave your turn indicator on all the time. It confuses people. I need you to be around for awhile."

"I'll be here," said Tyler. "Be sure and leave the light on."

"It's always on for you…Goodnight."

"Goodnight."

CHAPTER 7

FEAR OF DEATH

"There is no death. Only a change of worlds."
                                    Chief Seattle
"A death is but one night to the soul."
                                    Seth

"Well, at least you look a little more rested this week," I said.

"Nothing like a couple of pints of Type A blood to elevate the energy level."

"You found a plump little blond with vitamin-rich arterial blood?"

"Quite by accident. I was zipping down Colfax on my new scooter when…"

"Tyler, you're impossible."

"You say the nicest things, Edward. And I want to continue to be impossible for as long as I can. When people are gathered around the plastic urn containing my mortal remains, I want them to be saying, *You know, that Tyler, he was impossible right to the end.*"

"Plastic?"

"Yeah. Don't spend a lot of money on containers. It's a waste. Actually, if you can get biodegradable plastic it would be better. I don't know if that's a contradiction in terms—plastic and biodegradable. Anyway, get something that will decompose. I'll be back soon enough in a brand new container. Unless, of course, I get to go on to the next level."

"Didn't you tell me you had to be highly evolved to go on to the next level?

"True," said Tyler.

"Then don't worry, you'll be back."

"…Another vote of confidence from my fans."

"But wouldn't you rather have people say nice things about you? Like, *He was a wise and gentle soul*…At least something other than, *He was impossible right to the end.*"

"Spare me, Edward. That's much too serious."

"So, Maestro, what exactly would you like to have on your tombstone?"

"Well, first of all, I don't want a tombstone. I'd rather you scatter my ashes, at least part of them, on Legion Field up in Great Falls, Montana. You know, where the Dodger rookie team plays."

"Why there?"

"So I could spend at least some of the time watching rookies play baseball. Hear the kids, listen to the crowd. Play baseball bingo. I could watch the sixth inning bean bag toss and follow the little kids as they race around the bases. Maybe I could even see the Missouri River that flows not too far in back of the left field stands."

"That your idea of heaven? Rookie League baseball in Great Falls, Montana?"

"Something like that," said Tyler.

"Let's get back to the tombstone. If you did have one, what would you want on it?"

"I'd have to give it some thought."

"You'll tell me before you leave tonight?"

"You in a hurry to start the funeral services?"

"No, I was just curious about what…"

"I'll try to come up with something. Perhaps something witty and profound that people will quote for years to come …All of which brings us rather neatly into the subject for the evening—the fear of dying, the fear of pain."

"You afraid of dying, Maestro?"

"Not right now."

"Meaning?"

"I'm not afraid of dying at the moment, because I'm not actually dying right now. At the moment. At least that I know of."

"But you might be."

"Afraid or dying?" he said.

"…Both. Or either."

"I might be. *God gives the grace of death to the dying.* You ever hear that?"

"No."

"I can't remember where I heard it, but it makes sense. I believe that I'll get what I need when I get there."

"Another one of those grace things? Pumpkin Power?"

"Maybe. How about you and dying?"

"Frankly, I'm not all that cozy about it. It's not something I think about a lot."

"Somebody, maybe Ram Dass, says that you can't really live until you've practiced dying for awhile. Maybe it was Stephen Levine. And you know there are monks who sleep in coffins."

"That's a very morbid outlook, Tyler. I think you've been reading way too many of those thick spiritual books, the ones that have the Latin quotations they don't bother to translate. Try some light reading for a change."

"A blink of an eye, Edward, and it's gone."

"What is?"

"Life."

"God, you're depressing tonight."

"We're doing fears, Noble Student. Some actually are depressing. That's one of the reasons we talk about them; to give them some visibility, to demystify them, take some of the power away so they won't be hidden and control our lives in harmful ways."

"You said that when we started."

"Good. Shows how consistent I am. You less afraid of the dark now? I mean since we talked about it. Other people show up in your life who had similar fears?"

"Oddly enough, they did. Several people that I hardly knew started telling me about being afraid of the dark. I mean right out of the blue. I couldn't believe it."

"Believe, Edward. Believe. What about the fear of pain?"

"Tyler, everybody's afraid of those kinds of things. You're not going to tell me we're supposed to look forward to them...*I think I'll have that root canal without novocaine today, Doc. Practice up on my pain training.*"

"What do you think about when you think about dying?" said Tyler.

"I think about...suffocating. Being unable to breath. I get very claustrophobic and I start to hyperventilate. I picture thousands of little pie-shaped things that look like small piranha fish chewing on my lungs."

"You think about pain?" said Tyler.

"I don't think I want to even talk about this. Gives me the creeps. Pain. Death. Man..."

"Well, we could discuss lollipops or butterflies but we're actually talking about fears, Edward, and I don't know anyone who's afraid of lollipops or butterflies."

"Well...Okay. We'll leave the butterflies and lollipops out of it."

"So, when you think about dying, do you think about pain?"

"Sometimes. But I avoid it as a rule; even thinking about it, about pain. Most of the time I think about, oh...maybe my job, or some woman I've got my eye on, or a movie I want to see. A book. All very prosaic, Tyler. I don't get into those deep philosophical modes like you do. You know, where you're pondering the mysteries of the Universe while watching some ancient movie at the Gothic with Mercedes."

"You know what Mercedes says about dying?"

"No, what?"

"It's very safe," said Tyler.

"Dying is?"

"She said being born's a lot harder than dying."

"You think she knows?"

"I don't know."

"But you believe it. That it's safe. I can tell."

"I do."

"Why?"

"I don't know why, Edward. It has just always seemed to me that I could hardly wait to get off the planet. From the time I was little, I had this feeling that earth life wasn't for me, that somehow I just didn't belong. Life on Life's terms was far too painful to consider on a long term basis. I tried staying drunk all the time, but that didn't work. So dying seemed to be the only way out. Only I couldn't get anyone to cooperate and do it for me. Take a look at your own life. What do you think all those years of drinking and taking drugs were about?"

"Escape?"

"Good," said Tyler. "From what?"

"From...responsibility, stress, three marriages, all those jerks out there."

"From pain?"

"...Sure."

"From life?"

"Not all of it. Some of it's okay. Maybe even lots of it. It's not all Baywatch, but then it's not all Dr. Laura either. And the trouble with drinking or taking drugs was that I always overshot the mark. Once I started, I couldn't stop. Even when I wanted to. But that doesn't mean I'm ready to leave the planet yet. Maybe when I get as old as you are, I'll re-evaluate my position."

"It doesn't have anything to do with age, Edward."

"It doesn't?"

"No. Another mistaken notion about age. Actually, lots of people find life more precious than ever because there's less of it than there was. They want to hang on to what's left."

"I can relate to that."

"Don't make the mistake of missing the now by being afraid of the future. We spend far too much of our lives in either memory or anticipation. Some famous guy said that, *Life is like the lottery—must be present to win.* And fear, Noble Student, fear keeps us from living in the present."

"I get it. But what if there's nothing out there, Maestro? Out beyond the Veil as you tumble happily into the waiting arms of Morpheus? Or the Grim Reaper. Or whoever. What if there's nothing there."

"I've thought about that."

"Something to consider."

"What I've decided is that if there's nothing out there, I probably wouldn't know it. Doesn't Shakespeare say something about death being like a long sleep? *To die, to sleep, perchance to dream. . ."*

"I don't know. I'm rusty on my Shakespeare."

"So that'd be okay, too," said Tyler. "I like to sleep. But I know there's something more, Edward. Something more than this."

"And how do you know that, Maestro? You have inside information from the Great Pumpkin? From Mercedes? From Sources you haven't told me about?"

"Some things are just known in ways that I can't explain. Some things have no verbal equivalents. Actually, lots of things have no verbal equivalents. We labor under the illusion that if we don't have a name for it, it doesn't exist."

"And you attribute this, this knowledge you have about the Other Side to...what? Early neglect and abuse that sharpened your spiritual sensitivities? Alcoholism and drug addiction? Sleeping in a coffin when no one was looking? Monastic training from the years in prison that you seldom mention?"

"Pain, Edward. Pain is often the best teacher. There's a great line in The Varieties of Religious Experience that says:

> *The common denominator of deep spiritual experience is often pain and utter hopelessness.*

"What a cheery thought. So maybe I haven't suffered enough?"

"You're young yet," said Tyler. "Give Life a chance to beat you up a little more."

"And then I'll know?"

"You...might."

"I'll know that dying is very safe? And I won't be afraid."

"If you're anything like me," said Tyler, "you might have a fear of being sick, being unable to take care of yourself, which goes back to what we talked about in our last session. Maybe afraid that it will be painful. But you won't be afraid of dying because you'll realize, Noble Student, that nobody dies...*Like ships that sail out of sight, we just don't see them anymore.* The people who have died, that is. But they're still somewhere."

"Like over the rainbow? In the sweet by-and-by?"

"You could say that."

"What do you think it's like?" I said. "In the sweet by-and-by."

"I don't know that I have the vocabulary to describe it. I also don't know if I really know. But sometimes, during a quiet meditation, when I'm fortunate enough not to be thinking about myself, time seems to stop and something, some ...deep, peaceful space envelops me and I know, with every fiber of my being, that everything is okay, has always been okay, and there isn't anything I can do to screw it up. That I was born in a state of grace, that I will die in the same state, and nothing I can do in between will alter that fact. What happens is that I often fail to realize it. But be assured that all is well, Edward. Just breathe in and out, and watch the scenery. Enjoy the ride."

"Let it be noted that I'm shaking my head."

"It's like sitting on the floor and looking up at your mother doing some embroidery or needlepoint. All those..."

"What is...?"

"Life is...All those odd-colored threads and strings are hanging down and it doesn't look like anything that makes any sense. Then one day your mother lifts you up and you get a look at the other side and, *voila*, you can't believe how beautiful it is. It's a perfect picture of maybe a rose garden and suddenly it all makes sense. But you get only a brief glimpse and then you're down on the floor again looking up at this godawful odd collection of strings and threads. And as time goes by you wonder whether you actually saw the other side, or maybe just imagined the whole thing."

"Or maybe you just had a senior moment."

"Ah, my Noble Student."

"You ever hear voices?"

"I get...communications sometimes, but I wouldn't call them voices."

"That's really weird," I said. "Very weird."

"Isn't it, though."

"And just what am I supposed to do with all this information? Is this supposed to convince me that dying is actually user-friendly?"

"I'm not trying to convince you of anything, Edward. We've been over that. This is an equal opportunity issue. I'm sharing experience, strength and hope. That's all."

"I'm confused, Maestro."

"Good," said Tyler. "It's the beginning of wisdom."

"Confusion is?"

"Indeed."

"You realize this is our last session?"

"For now," he said.

"I'll miss them."

"Me, too. I think of them as explorations, scouting expeditions into some...strange and wonderful world that's too big for words."

"What is it you think we're looking for?"

"Some kind of light. Something to chase away the shadows and the fears."

"The old enlightenment routine?" I said.

"There's a wisdom saying that goes...

Gaining enlightenment is an accident—spiritual practice makes us accident prone.

"And your definition of spiritual practice is...?"

94

"Having a chat with the Great Pumpkin in the morning, resting in His or Her presence, trying to create some space where I'm not constantly thinking about myself—how I'm doing, how I look, what people think of me. Once I heard a guy say...*I may not be much, but I'm all I think about.*"

"Sounds familiar. I'm guilty of that on occasion."

"Unfortunately, nearly all of us are."

"What's the cure?"

"You already know the answer, Edward. The first order of business is being of service. Get your phone list out and call people and ask how *they* are. Go to detox and tell them it's possible to live without drugs and alcohol. And you know because you're doing it. Go to the hospice and sit with someone who's dying. Just be there. See if your neighbor needs anything. You don't have to look far because basically everyone's your neighbor. Think of the people you see every day with no teeth, scotch-taped glasses, tangle-wood hair, eyes that have that thousand yard stare, hands that are cracked and grimy pushing shopping carts with wobbly wheels. Take an action. There's lots of lonely people out there."

"It's Tyler, the action guy."

"You ever notice that nearly all the problems have the same remedy—do something for someone else. And there's really no need to worry about dying, Edward. As far as I know, nobody's getting out of this thing alive anyway. There will be people to help you."

"Will you be there?"

"I will," said Tyler. "I'll be on the Other Side leading the parade."

"We're having a parade?"

"A welcoming parade in your honor. The banner will say, *Welcome Home, Edward.*"

"And I won't be afraid?"

95

"How could you be afraid? You'll be *home*. Then I'll take you to a meeting. Your real home group…I ever tell you the joke about the two old baseball players in the nursing home?"

"Somehow I missed that one."

"These two old guys make a deal. Whichever one dies first the other one comes back to tell him what it's like. So Tyler goes first and…"

"The guy's name is Tyler?"

"This is a story, Edward…So Tyler goes first and three days later he appears at the foot of Edward's bed and he says, *I got some good news and some bad news, Eddy. The good news is they got baseball every day, doubleheaders every weekend…What's the bad news, says Eddy…And Tyler says, You're pitchin' next Tuesday.*"

"You are truly impossible."

"High praise," said Tyler. "Just remember that the journey is safe."

"So you're out into the night?"

"I am. Laundry and to bed."

"That's all?"

"That's all. I ever tell you about the poem I wrote when I was in the eighth grade?"

"No," I said. "And why am I just finding out all these things about you now?"

"I guess because now is the time. The poem goes like this…

> *Now I lay me down to die*
> *And pray that in the morning I*
> *Will never have to wake and see*
> *A single thing, not even me.*

"You wrote that when you were in the eighth grade?"

"I did."

"Tyler, I'm not ready to have you leave yet."

"Don't worry," he said. "I'll be here through the weekend at least."

"I'm counting on a longer time frame."

"You know what I'd like to have on my tombstone? If I was going to have a tombstone?

"What?"

"Thank you," said Tyler.

"That's it? Thank you?"

"That's it. Which will include a Thank You to The Great Pumpkin for allowing me to take the journey, to my children who taught me so much, to the Community who nurtured me, to those who allowed me to love them and loved me in return."

"Man..."

I couldn't say anything more for a few seconds. Sometimes I get a little choked up when the weather's cold. Like it is now.

"Goodnight, Tyler...I love you. May the Force be with you."

"And with you, Noble Student. As It always is. And know that the love is returned a hundred fold...Just remember that the sun is always shining. Always. Sometimes there are clouds that get in the way, but the sun is always there whether you can see it or not. And as you progress along the Path, as you take action, there will be fewer clouds. And more sun."

"Goodnight...And don't you dare leave yet."

"...Goodnight, Edward. I won't leave without telling you first."

ABOUT THE AUTHOR

Edward Bear is a pseudonym. The author was born in Brooklyn, New York and grew up in Los Angeles, California. Early adventures included a brief stint in minor league baseball, too many years in construction, day labor and other dead-end jobs. He attended six colleges, received no degrees. A correspondence course in engineering landed him a job at Hewlett Packard where he was employed for nearly thirty years.

Previous publications: several fiction pieces in small literary magazines and journals; a baseball novel, *DIAMONDS ARE TRUMPS*, St. Luke's Press (1990), *THE DARK NIGHT OF RECOVERY, Conversations from the Bottom of the Bottle*, Health Communications, Inc. (1999); *THE SEVEN DEADLY NEEDS*, Health Communications, Inc. (2000), and *THE COCKTAIL CART*, M & J Publishing (2001). The elusive Mr. Bear currently lives in the Rocky Mountains with his wife, plays a vintage Martin guitar and writes in whatever time the gods and goddesses have left him.

To contact the author—www.edwardbear.net
or
edbear01@aol.com

ORDER FORM

Please send____copies of THE SEVEN DEADLY FEARS
@ $9.95 plus shipping to:

Name:_____

Street:_____

City:_____

State:_____Zip:_____

Colorado residents add 7.2% sales tax (72 cents per book).

____Books at $9.95...$_____
Shipping..$_____
Tax (if Colorado resident)................................$_____
Total.......$_____

Shipping:
First Class: $3.50 for the first book and 75 cents for each
additional book.

Send check or money order to:

M&J Publishing
P.O. Box 460516
Denver, CO 80246-0516
        (Make checks payable to M&J Publishing)

**If you do not have the money to purchase the book, just
send in the order form and the book will be mailed to you
without charge.**